Wait Till You See Me Dance

P9-DMR-300

Also by Deb Olin Unferth

Revolution: The Year I Fell in Love and Went to Join the War
Vacation
Minor Robberies

Wait Till You See Me Dance

Stories

DEB OLIN UNFERTH

Graywolf Press

This publication is made possible, in part, by the voters of Minnesota through a Minnesota State Arts Board Operating Support grant, thanks to a legislative appropriation from the arts and cultural heritage fund, and through grants from the National Endowment for the Arts and the Wells Fargo Foundation. Significant support has also been provided by Target, the McKnight Foundation, the Amazon Literary Partnership, and other generous contributions from foundations, corporations, and individuals. To these organizations and individuals we offer our heartfelt thanks.

Published by Graywolf Press
250 Third Avenue North, Suite 600
Minneapolis, Minnesota 55401

All rights reserved.

www.graywolfpress.org

Published in the United States of America

ISBN 978-1-55597-768-9

2 4 6 8 9 7 5 3 1
First Graywolf Printing, 2017

Library of Congress Control Number: 2016938178

Cover design: Kimberly Glyder Design

Cover image: Shutterstock

For Matt

Contents

1

Likable   5
Pet   7
Wait Till You See Me Dance   18
Stay Where You Are   42

2

To the Ocean   63
The Vice President of Pretzels   65
Defects   67
A Crossroads   69
An Opera Season   71
How to Dispel Your Illusions   74
Granted   76
My Daughter Debbie   77
Open Water   81
The Applicant   84
The Walk   86
Online   88
Your Character   90
Fear of Trees   92

3

Voltaire Night   95

Mr. Simmons Takes a Prisoner   114

The First Full Thought of Her Life   125

Bride   139

4

Husband   153

The Mothers   154

Final Days   157

Decorate, Decorate   159

37 Seconds   160

Interview   163

Flaws   164

The One Fondly Mentioned   165

Draft   167

Welcome   168

Boulder   171

The Last Composer   172

Yesterday   174

Abandon Normal Instruments   175

The Magicians   180

Dirty Joke (in translation)   183

Mr. Creativity   185

Wait Till You See Me Dance

1

Likable

She could see she was becoming a thoroughly unlikable person. Each time she opened her mouth she said something ugly, and whoever was nearby liked her a little less. These could be strangers, these could be people she loved, or people she knew only slightly whom she had hoped would one day be her friends. Even if she didn't say anything, even if all she did was *seem* a certain way, have a look on her face, or make a soft sound of reaction, what she did was always unlikable—except in the few cases when she fixed herself on being likable for the next four seconds (more than that was impossible), and sometimes that worked, but not always.

Why couldn't she be more likable? What was the problem? Did she just not enjoy the world anymore? Had the world gotten away from her? Had the world gotten worse? (Maybe, probably not. Or probably in some ways but not in the ways that were making her not like it.) Did she not like herself? (Well, of course she didn't, but there was nothing new in that.)

Or had she become less likable simply by growing older—so that she might be doing the same thing she had always done, but because she was now forty-four, not twenty, it had become unlikable because any woman doing something at forty-four is more unlikable than a woman doing it at twenty? And does she sense this? Does she know she is intrinsically less likable and instead of resisting, does she lean into it, as into a cold wind? Maybe (likely) she used to resist, but now she sees the futility, so each morning when she opens her mouth she is unlikable, proudly so, and each evening before sleep she is unlikable, and each day it goes on this way, she turning more unlikable by the hour, until one morning she will be so unlikable, inconveniently unlikable, that she will have to be shoved into a hole and left there.

Pet

Somehow they have wound up with these two turtles. The woman says she saved them. Her son says all she did was move them from one place to another—from the basement of her sister's house to their apartment (also a basement)—and the turtles' lives are no better than they were before, and her own life is significantly worse, since now she has to take care of them.

Well, the woman and her son will take care of them together.

Not him. He's not the one who took them. He doesn't even know why she did it—making off with somebody's pets? That's weird.

Those turtles would have died down there in the dark, like all the other pets in her sister's life. It was a philanthropic moment, taking them. It's called philanthropy. Does he even know what that is? she wonders.

Besides, the turtles aren't much work. She has to feed them and check the water temperature and turn their light on and off. She has to clean the tank each week. She has to take the tank's water out, cup by cup, pour it into a bowl, then carry the bowl to the tub, walk through two rooms to do it (drops of dirty water falling on the floor). She has to empty bowl after bowl. She doesn't know how many bowls fill a tank. Many. And many cups to fill a bowl. Another way to do it is by siphon. She could put the siphon in her mouth, suck, and when she sees the water coming up, pour it into the bowl.

Are you kidding me, putting that turtle shit in your mouth? says her son.

Since when does he use words like that and at his mother too.

Can I use words like salmonella? says her son. Can I use words like incredibly stupid?

Another question: when was the last time someone actually touched this woman, not counting the turtles? A long time.

She wound up with the turtles in the first place because every time she looked in the basement that week she saw the turtles. One of her house-sitting jobs for her sister was to feed them. Really, the situation was so pathetic. You'd go down to the darkest, coldest basement, make your way toward a corner that had a little light, and there would be two turtles, one sitting on top of the other because they had only one rock, and it was bad. You'd toss in a few food sticks and think, Okay, this is why we will all go to hell. Or think, Well, God did put us in charge of things, right? Or think, What was God thinking? Or think, What were the owners of this house—her own sister and that God-awful husband of hers—thinking? Who are these people that they could leave these little animals down here with their long frowns? So she called her sister in Florida and said, There are two turtles in the basement, and I have to say they don't look very pleased.

Do you know how long turtles live? said the sister. Do you know what it's like to have kids who one day come home with one turtle and then another day come home with another, and you get to be either the mom who will let them have turtles or the mom who won't? And then guess who's stuck taking care of them for the next hundred years?

By all means, said the sister, I'm sure you'd do a better job. Take them. Take everything—tank, food, thermometer, rock. Get them out of my house.

Now one of the turtles is sick or something is wrong with it. It just lies on the bottom of the tank, not moving—see that? How it's lying there? It could drown.

Don't look at him, says her son. He's just leaving, just out the door.

Was she looking at him? Would he like to report where her eyes were resting at the moment of the observation? Was it on the tank or him? And don't forget how much he always said he wanted a pet.

He wanted a pet when he was eight.

The turtle could drown.

Well, she's responsible for it, he says. It was her philanthropic moment that led her into this and he's not going to be the one to lead her out. If he were her, he would first toss the turtle out into the courtyard and vow never to have another philanthropic moment again. Then he would go out to the courtyard and find the turtle and bring it to the vet.

So she does all that and she waits her turn and then the vet says he has no idea. He's a vet for mammals, he says. He puts the turtle on a scale and says, Its weight is fine! And the nurse and the other people around there laugh. He pulls on its little legs and measures it and says, Well, it's long enough! And the nurses laugh again.

It's all a big waste of her time and embarrassing, and it costs forty bucks. Then she has to carry the turtle in a tool case all day because she's worried it might die in the tank while she's gone. She takes the turtle to work and puts it under her desk by her feet and then she takes it to her AA meeting. She opens the case a little because she's worried it might suffocate inside.

What is that thing? someone at the AA meeting says. That is really ugly.

She looks down at it. True, it's not the nicest-looking animal, but how many creatures of the earth can honestly say that they are, including this person before her?

People gather around. What's wrong with it? they say.

It's covered in mud, they say.

The shell just looks like that, she says. It just looks that way.

You can't have that in here, they say.

It's just a turtle, a new man says.

The others look at him. It may have a disease, they say. Get that thing out of here.

She takes the case and leaves.

She sits at the kitchen table with her head in her arms. Her son comes in and says she could leave the turtle out in the street. Maybe a car would come along and hit it.

The turtle doesn't get better. She calls the pet store, calls her sister, calls other people she knows who have pets or who are generally responsible people. No one has any idea. No one knows, until finally someone says, Oh, I know. It needs those vitamin flakes and a special light so it can absorb nutrients. So she goes out and buys the special light and the vitamin flakes and they are expensive and the store is far and she sees she has a ticket on her car when she comes out, but lo and behold, the turtle is better in a few days or at least swimming around like before.

No thanks to her son, who couldn't help her with one little thing.

No thanks to her son, who couldn't manage to get home at a decent hour. Here it is, nearly midnight. Where is he? She goes up in her robe to the entryway to see if he is lying dead in the street. The security door is propped open with a brick, so anyone could come in and kill them. She stands looking out into the dark to see if her son is being held up on the corner, or being stabbed or shot. A man comes in who isn't her son.

Are you the one who propped this door open? she says. So anyone can come in here?

I'm a single woman living alone with my son, she says.

The man shrugs. So get a husband, he says.

Her son appears at 2 a.m. Have you been drinking? she says, following him down the hall. Just tell me that.

A tall glass of shut-the-fuck-up, he says and goes into his room.

She can't do this, just can't. She's not equipped to deal with small animals, teenagers, basement apartments. She calls her sister. Do you think your kids want their turtles back?

Oh no you don't, her sister says. I don't care what you do with those turtles but don't bring them here. I'm the good guy for once. Their aunt stole them—it wasn't anything I did.

I saved them, says the woman.

I think you were looking in the wrong basement.

She hadn't been the best mom. She knows that. There were a few rough years. He used to want to be with her all the time. Now he avoids her.

Do you want to go shopping on Saturday? she says.

Do I want to sit in traffic for hours with only you to talk to? Not likely.

Go to the movies, then? Dinner?

Look, Mom, you're not my date. Okay? And we're not friends. You're the parent. I'm the kid who suffers in your presence until I can get away.

She never left him chained to a radiator or locked in a closet. She did leave him with friends a couple of times, once when he had the chicken pox, once when she went into detox. Twice. Once on Halloween.

With no costume, her son says.

But it worked out all right, didn't it? You like Ron and Cici. Ron and Cici are very nice people.

At least they weren't drunk, if that's what you mean.

They liked you. They took you trick-or-treating. You got a pumpkin full of candy.

They felt sorry for me. My mother was a drunk.

They bought you a costume.

Of a superhero nobody ever heard of, he says.

And another thing, he says. You didn't leave me with them. I called them. They came and picked me up.

But now that the turtle is better it keeps fighting with the other turtle, the smaller one, hurting it, snapping at it, its friend, the only one it may ever have and some have less than that, and still the turtle keeps biting. And it is really sad because the smaller one wants to be near the bigger one all the time, can't rest unless it is next to the bigger one, who keeps biting it each time it gets close. So she calls all the same people again and they say they have no idea again and she thinks this is going to go on eternally. She'll always have a question no one can answer and a long list of people to ask. She goes to an AA meeting and talks about it, and they, too, look bored, wishing she'd go away. Finally the new man says, Sounds like you need a second tank. Or one less turtle. Why don't you take one to the pet store?

It has been so long since anyone gave her advice that she wanted to hear, she is tearful with gratitude.

We can't take that, the clerk at the pet store says.

Oh please, she says. I'll pay you.

Sorry. Why don't you take it to the reptile swap?

What's that?

It turns out there's a place you go to bring your reptile if you don't want it anymore and are willing to take another one home. Maybe she could get a frog or a fish, a pet that lives less long. It's very far and it's illegal so she takes the turtle in a hatbox, drives out on the toll road on a Saturday. The reptile swap is held in a muddy field, which she hadn't understood would be the case. She is wearing high heels. Her shoes sink when she steps and she can feel water seeping through the soles. She wants a drink. It's hard to walk and she wobbles with her hatbox. People look at her strangely. She carries the hatbox from table to table. Nobody wants her turtle. They have chirping dragons, six-foot snakes. There's a single tiny monkey gripping the bars of its cage like a convict. No one looks at her turtle. She brings it back home.

Monday she finds a note on her desk: *Were you going to send out the minutes before leaving for the weekend? Never mind, I did it. P.S. I'm writing this at 9:15, did I forget you were coming in late today?*

She wonders, Why do other people have pets? Is it for the same bad reason as she? What is her bad reason? She doesn't know. They aren't even cute, the turtles, this one especially. It looks like an oven mitt. She feels nothing for these turtles. She hates them. They are ugly. They smell bad.

Now she has two tanks and she has to clean two of them and it is awful. She hates it so much that she waits and waits until the water is cloudy and polluted and stinks. Finally she begins dumping out the water, carrying both tanks' worth of water across two rooms to the bathroom and pouring it into the tub, but there is so much shit in it, it clogs. A puddle of brown water in the tub.

Oh God, what is she going to do now? There's shit in the tub.

You put it in the tub? her son calls from his room. Shit goes in the toilet, Mom.

Oh God, why is this happening? Why does everything she does turn out this way? There is no way out of this. This is hell. And you know what? She is supposed to have a date tonight, the only one in, what, a year? Two years?

A what? her son comes out of his room to say. What did you just say?

Yes, she has a date. With a man from a meeting.

One of those drug addicts, those drunks?

Yes, well, after she was forced to leave with the turtle in the tool case and was crying in the parking lot holding the turtle case in one hand and her purse in the other, the new man came out and said, Let's see what you've got there? And she showed him. At the next meeting he said something nice about her remarks and at the next meeting he sat next to her and asked if he could bring her a cup of coffee when he went to get his own cup, and after that he asked after the turtles and after her son, and at the next meeting he asked if she wanted to go to dinner.

And you said *yes?*

And she said yes. So basically she has a date and she is trying to hurry it up with these tanks, and dirty water keeps splashing onto the floor and now the tub is clogged. And yes, the man is a little old for her and not as good-looking as her son's father and is maybe not going to win any awards for being dashing and rich, but anyway it is more or less a date.

When were you going to tell me? her son says. What the fuck is going on? How old is this guy who's a little old for her—eighty?

So she goes and buys some drain cleaner, the really powerful stuff. She pours it in and waits (You didn't mention any man, says her son, didn't say a word. Well, she does have other concerns on her mind just now) and the drain explodes. Turtle feces all over the tub and the wall and the curtain and the window because that is the kind of place she lives in with her only son, a basement apartment with cheap drains in a bad neighborhood because her husband divorced her and left, even though she stopped drinking, and he never calls his son, not even on his birthday, never sends enough money, and there is turtle shit on the wall and she has to be up early, and meanwhile years are going by, her son growing up and she fading further from his mind.

There's turtle shit everywhere, her son is saying. And you're bringing home drunks. This place has got to be unfit. Who do I call to report you? I should go live with Dad.

Go ahead, she says. If you can get him on the phone.

How has she come to this? How? She can put a heroic spin on it or a negative one. She could make herself look enlightened or close to tramphood. She has never seen a woman make worse choices than she. She has never known any person so transparently wrongheaded, so obviously in need of job counseling, parenting classes, therapy, help of any kind, any lifeboat, any raft, so obviously in need of a hard, careful look at herself, and so obviously not going to do it. She is that unaware. That full of the opposite of insight, that doomed to middling livelihood at best, certain solitude, early illness, weakness, not-quite poverty, strained relations with her son, relatives who don't really like her taking care of her when she is old. The indignity of all this, the shame. How exhausting, this life, this topic, how senseless, how difficult. She has her face in her hands. And what is that now—turtle shit in her hair? Well, this is a lovely way to spend the afternoon. Does she feel better now, Miss Pity Party? The phone rings. That would be her date.

Don't answer that, her son says.

She reaches for the phone.

Don't you dare, her son says. You're going to go out with that drug addict and leave me here in this shit?

All right, all right, she says. She picks up the phone. I can't go, she says to the man on the phone. I'm sorry. I can't go out.

Come on, says the man on the phone. You need a night out.

She tells him about the turtle shit. She is standing in the bathroom doorway looking at it.

I'm coming over, says the man on the phone.

No, her son says. He is behind her. Tell that guy he better not show up.

I'll help you clean it up, says the man on the phone.

What? she says.

Sure, I don't mind.

Do you know what we're talking about here? she says. Have you been drinking?

He's been drinking, says her son. Tell him not to come.

I'm on my way, I'm in the car, he says. I've got all the supplies in the back.

Don't come. My son's in hysterics.

WHAT, her son screams.

We'll drive them to the turtle pond.

What turtle pond? she says.

WHAT TURTLE POND? her son says.

There's a turtle pond, hundreds of turtles. They line up on the logs like dots. Turtles that used to have owners like you. Owners who visit each spring, they bring binoculars. They ride out on the pond in canoes.

I don't have any canoe.

WE HATE CANOES, her son says.

We'll go in the spring. The turtles will walk through the grass. They'll dive bravely into the water.

They'll be the ones who get to set me free, she says.

Wait Till You See Me Dance

1.

I know when people will die. I meet them, I can look into their faces and see if they have long to last. It's like having a knack for math or a green thumb, both of which I also have. People wear their health on their faces.

There was a time I lived alone in the crappiest neighborhood I would ever live in and had few friends and worked at a place where the people I saw were all quietly abandoning their plans, like I was. I had the faces of dying people all around me. One day the office assistant called me over to her desk and said she was an Indian dancer and how would I like to go to an Indian dance?

This same office assistant had once said to me, "You know what I think every time I look at you? Guess. Guess what I think."

"Here comes the bride," I said.

"Wrong," she said. "I think about that movie where the angel comes to earth and shows a man the future and how bad it's going to be, and the man looks at the future and says, 'But what about Mary? What happens to her?' And the angel says, 'You're not going to like it, George.' And George says, 'Well, I have to know. Tell me, Angel.' And the angel says, 'She's an old maid! She works at the library!' And the man says, 'Nooooooo!'"

"I don't know that movie," I said.

"'She's an old maid! She works at the library!' You should put that on your voice mail."

"I don't work at the library."

"People would know they had the right number."

After that she called me Mary and soon had them all calling me Mary.

This office assistant sat at her desk and handed out notices about forms that people had forgotten to fill out. She wrote down on slips of paper chore lists, reminders, disclosures she'd received from above: *Tag your food. Turn in your book orders. You have been chosen for a special assignment.* I didn't like her. She was young and hard to talk to and not nice. She wasn't the only office assistant. There were two others, who were locked in an eternal battle and fought every single day. A partition had been raised between them in the hope that if they didn't see each other they would each cease to believe in the other's existence. It hadn't worked. All it did was make them think they each had their own office, which they protected fiercely. The entire setup was confusing and inconvenient. If you wanted anything done, you had to depend on the first office assistant, the one who had asked me to the dance.

So this assistant was a lot of things but she certainly was not Indian, and on the day she asked me to the dance I said so. "What kind of an Indian are you supposed to be?" I said. Then it turned out she meant Native American—or American Indian. But she wasn't that either.

"You have the cheeks of a cowgirl," I said. "You have the face of a cowboy." It was true. She was both pretty and masculine.

Well, she had learned how to dance some Native American dances and her own mother had sewn her a Native American costume. It was beautiful, the costume, she said, and if you drove out of the city, you could find the land the Native Americans once lived on and still do today and where they dance still. She had a flyer about it, look.

"I never heard of this place," I said.

"Do you want to come or not?"

"I don't know how to dance any Native American dances."

"They'll teach you, everyone will. They're very nice out there."

I didn't know why she wanted me along. Maybe she wanted more friends, which might not be so bad considering the way things were going just then.

"Okay," I said. "I'll go."

"Great," she said. Her eyebrows went up. "You'll drive? I don't have a car."

At this job, four times a day, thirty people assembled before me, and it was my duty to tell them some useful fact about the English language, a fact they could then take and go out into the world with and use to better their positions in society. There were no grades in the class. It was a pass/fail class and whether they got a "pass" or a "fail" depended on an essay they had to write on the last day, which was read and evaluated by outside sources. These outside sources were supposed to be mysterious, were maybe not even people, were maybe just God, but I happened to know were simply whichever teacher or two the office assistant lined up to do it. It was a probationary class, intended for the students so illiterate that it was almost unseemly to have them there. It was the last-chance class. It went by the number 99. Anyone who passed got to enter college for real, sign up for 101. Anyone who failed had to leave. The students from 99 were all over the hallways. They didn't care about any useful facts to take out into the world. They cared only about the essay graded by outside sources. Thirty percent failed most years and everybody knew this. The students in 99 disliked me with a vigor and a courage that were kind of amazing. I stood at the front of the room on Mondays, Wednesdays, and Fridays, and said, "The test is graded by outside sources." I used this to respond to every complaint, defense, and plea.

The test is graded by outside sources.

The test is graded by outside sources.

The test is graded by outside sources.

That day, after I agreed to bring the assistant to the dance, I went and stood in front of my third class of the day. It was nearly the end of the semester and they had that unstrung look to them—gaunt, spooked, blaming. "Let me remind you," I told them, "I don't grade the tests. And I can tell you this much. Any essay without a proper introduction will not get a 'pass,' so let's turn our attention back to the board."

I was what is called an adjunct: a thing attached to another thing in a dependent or subordinate position.

The assistant had it a little wrong about the movie, by the way. It wasn't the future that George got to see. The angel's job is to show George what the world would be like if George had never existed. The premise of the movie—because of course I'd seen it, everyone's seen it, if you were born in America you've seen it—is that George is unhappy and has been for many years, his whole life nearly, and he is so full of regret and fear that he wants to die, or, even better, not to have been born in the first place.

2.

Some months before the assistant asked me to the dance, the associate chair called me into his office. This was a man whose face held the assurance of the living: he'd hold up a good long while yet.

"Do you have room in any of your classes?" he said.

"No," I said, "I don't have any room. I certainly don't have room two weeks into the semester."

"I'm sorry to hear that, Mary, because we've got this kid here." He pointed to a kid in the corner whom I hadn't noticed yet. A thin boy who clutched several plastic grocery bags to his chest.

"My name's not Mary," I said.

"It's not?"

"He missed two weeks," I said. "Forget it."

"He's here on a visa."

"Does he speak any English?" I said.

We looked at him. He looked back at us as if he might startle himself off his chair.

"Take the kid," the associate chair said.

Once a visa student in 99 wrote me a poem about how much I was helping him improve his grammar. One of the lines of the poem went:

Thou laid really strong excellent basement.

The kid was a worse-than-average 99 student. He couldn't write a sentence. He turned in his first jumbled essay and I thought: There is no way this kid is going to pass. And I thought: What a bother for him to fly all the way across the world to sit in my class and then to fly back home. And by the time I finished those two thoughts he was already shifting to the back of my mind, he was already taking a seat amid the blur of other students, whose names I would never know, whose faces I'd forget, and whose passing or failing grades were like changes in the air temperature, were nothing to do with me.

Every semester I went through this. I'd had the job two years. I had local city kids and a few foreign students, all of them ready for certain destruction. Some brought me fruit baskets. Some tried to bribe me into passing them. One threatened me, told me his "alliances" would look me up one day.

By the third week of the semester what this kid was to me was nothing to do with me.

By accident I heard him play. I was walking down the hallway toward another tedious day and a strange sound stopped me. Strands of violin and piano were coming from behind a door. I looked in.

Did I mention that this run-down school, this flat barrel-bottom place, was run between the walls of a building designed by a very famous architect? Yes, it was. It had been the high point of the architect's career. It was while making this building that the architect had come up with his very best ideas about designing buildings and had summed these ideas up in a short catchy sentence that he said aloud and that was later written into books that were read all over the world and that was now familiar even to the layperson. After saying this catchy sentence, the architect succumbed to his drinking problem and never straightened himself out and eventually died bankrupt and alone, but this building still stood, and now somehow these people had gotten their hands on the place and were ruining it as fast as they could. Water damage, broken tiles, missing doorknobs, and, worst of all, modern rehab: linoleum floors, drop ceilings, paint over wood. Catastrophe was setting in, but this one room had been preserved—perhaps because the public still encountered it on festive holiday occasions. The architect's one mistake had been to put this room on the seventh floor. The public had to be ushered in past the wreckage to reach it, up the new fake-wood-paneled elevators, over the colorless hallway carpet that had been nailed down there. But once inside, an auditorium opened up overhead and it was flawless. It marked that thin line of one artistic movement shifting into another, one great artist at his best.

On the stage the kid from my class was on the piano. Another student was playing the violin. The kid kept lifting one hand, keeping the left hand going and conducting the violin with his melody hand. Then the violin stopped and the kid continued to play and the sound I was hearing was formal and sad and peculiar. I myself had studied piano for years. I'd wanted to be a concert pianist in high school, which is its own separate bad joke now, but I knew this guy was super good. The piece had a density and a mathematical oddness, an originality. He stopped playing and looked up. I ducked out the door.

I stood in the hallway, thinking. How had such a talented kid wound up at our school? The school was no great music school. There were better music schools up the street, not to mention all over the country and the world.

I felt like I couldn't breathe for a moment, like my lungs were being pressed. I saw the emotional deadness in me and I saw it lift. It was temporarily gone.

Another paper of his landed in the pile. I couldn't understand any of it. Something about cars. The color of cars. Maybe about the color of cars. Something about the advent of America, of bank machines and microwave sandwiches. That afternoon he sat in the back of the class, wrote down whatever was going up on the board. I told him to talk to me at the end of the hour. He came and stood in front of me, his plastic bags in his hands at his sides. He was the same height as me, and he had sharp, dark good looks, though his nervousness shaded them. "Yes, miss?" he said.

"Why don't you explain to me what you're trying to say here," I said. I had his paper in my hand, and he lifted his eyebrows over it.

"Is it not right?" he said.

I dropped the paper onto the desk. "This writing is horrendous," I said. "What are you doing at this school? Didn't you apply anywhere else? Proper music schools?"

He said nothing.

Suddenly I was overwhelmed. "Well?" I said. "Well?"

The room was washed-out that day. Even the fluorescents were dim.

"You're never going to pass this class," I said.

He turned and walked toward the door.

"I heard you in the auditorium," I said, shaking. "I saw you."

He stopped at the door and looked back at me.

You think it's so easy doing what's right?

Once I had a student from Mexico who'd crossed the Rio Grande over and over and had always been caught. At one point he'd been lost for three days and nights, alone in the Texas desert. He'd thought it was the end of him for sure. At last he found a road and thought, My God, I am saved. The first car that came down the road was border patrol. He was back in Mexico in an hour. Another time he had tried to cross and had been sent back and had been so frustrated that he decided to use all his money and fly to Canada that same day, which he did. I don't know why he didn't just stay in Canada. I never asked him that. What's so bad about Canada? But he had that American addiction, I guess. He tried to cross at Niagara Falls, had been caught again, and was sent back again—so two times from two sides of the country in thirty-nine hours. Well, he'd made it to the United States at last and the only reason he wanted to be here, he said, was to get an education. ("What, they don't have schools in Mexico?" I'd said, and he'd been annoyed.) Here in the United States he'd gotten fake papers, he told me. He'd gotten a job with those papers, was working under a fake name. The job paid for him to go to college, so he was getting a degree under a fake name and would have to give up his identity forever, but he didn't care. If he didn't pass the class, the college would make him leave and the job wouldn't pay for school anymore.

He didn't pass.

Frankly, I knew it didn't matter if he passed or not, because I knew he wouldn't live for long. I had no idea how he would die but I knew.

I went into the chair's office to find this kid's file. The music kid, not the Mexican kid.

"What are you doing in there?" the office assistant called to me. "You're not supposed to be in there." She followed me in and watched me pull open a cabinet drawer.

"Those are confidential," she said. "That is strictly administrative."

"I need to see something." I took out the kid's file.

"What do you need to see?" she said, coming up behind me and leaning over my shoulder. "You don't get to see."

"Could you shut up for two seconds? For God's sake."

The name of his country was at the top of his file and it surprised me. It happened that his country was in a civil war that year. We'd been bombing them for reasons that had become suspect. It was all over the news. It was a mess.

The file had several notes in it. There was his acceptance date and his refusal letter. He'd received scholarships from several schools. He'd not chosen our school, the letter said. But thank you. Next there was a note from admissions, dated a year later. He wanted to come after all. He'd lost his scholarship from the school of his choice. He hadn't been able to get out of his country. He was of drafting age. There was a freeze on his passport. But this year, this *week,* there was a temporary reprieve. He could leave if he had sponsorship. Would we sponsor him? The date of the note put it two weeks into the semester, three days before he'd joined my class.

Any other school would have said, Come spring semester, come next year. But he couldn't come next year. It was leave then or be drafted and surely die. Probably his second choice and third choice had refused him. Fourth choice. Who knows how low on the list we lay. All I know is our school said they would take him—not out of generosity, it seemed from the paperwork, but sheer incompetence. If he failed this class, he'd have to go back, sign up for the war like everybody else.

The odd thing was, I looked at him, and I couldn't get a read on him. He could live another month, or he could live eighty more years.

I went to his musical-composition teacher and asked him what he planned to do about this kid.

"'Do?'" said the composition teacher. "Explain 'do.' Can you guess how many students I have?" he wanted to know. "Look, I'm not a blood donor. Do I look like a blood donor?"

"I'm an adjunct too," I said.

"Okay. You know what I'm talking about."

The adjuncts were always tired. Our classes were over-enrolled. The school didn't give us health insurance. Every year there was a Christmas party and the adjuncts were never invited. All the adjuncts shared one big office in a space like a spaceship, full of desks and boxes and books. We worked under contract and we were paid nearly nothing. Below minimum wage. People were shocked when they found out how much I made. I hated the other adjuncts, some younger, some older, each with their own cowardly reason for being there. And I hated the associate chair and the smug new-world music he played with his suburban band on weekends, and how he assigned me 99 semester after semester, somehow slotted me in there without even knowing my name. And I hated myself for hating all these perfectly reasonable citizens who were just going about their lives.

I needed to just pass him myself. Put a big P on his paper and move him through.

I guess I was in love with him a little. I didn't want him to go back.

I wasn't used to being in love, not with anyone and certainly not with a student, certainly not one eleven years younger than I, one I barely spoke to. It was horrible. I had to wait for our class and then hope to see him in the hallway beforehand, maybe walk in at the same moment, and I had to wonder whether he'd be going to some performance at the school that night and therefore whether I should go too. I had to puzzle out where he'd be rehearsing and which group he hung around with (the other foreign musicians: the Chileans, the Russians, the Japanese) and where they might be and whether I could sometimes be nearby, watching. I tried to do an especially good job in his class. I stopped reading aloud from the textbook. I required the students to visit the writing center. The papers came back even worse.

I was giving it up, had given it up. He wasn't even going to pass the class.

"That's some lousy job you've got."

This was the office assistant talking. I was stapling sheets of paper together. I was pulling out staples from papers I had incorrectly stapled and restapling the papers to the correct ones. I looked over at her and could suddenly see that she was doomed. I could see it as clearly and abruptly as if I'd reached over and stapled right through her jugular, put six staples into her neck.

"What else do you do," she said, "walk dogs? Clean up their crap? This job's not for you. You should quit."

A staple lodged under my fingernail. "Hey," I said, "do you have anyone lined up to do the essays yet?"

"What essays?"

"The 99s."

"Oh, crap. I was going to bribe someone."

"I'll do it."

"No one wants to do it."

"Put me down."

"I can't put you down."

"Go ahead. Put me down."

"Can't do that. You're not an outside source."

She was right about that. The outside sources weren't from outside the school or the country or the planet but from outside 99. The 101 teachers read the 99s. The 205 teachers.

I said, "Who checks? Does anybody check?"

"I check. I'm supposed to check."

"Don't check."

"I'm not putting you down."

I was surprised by this. In previous semesters, I'd been on the receiving end of mass emails begging someone to volunteer. Anyone not teaching 99 could expect to get asked to come in on the last Saturday of final-exam week. I had thought it would be easy to convince her, that she would be relieved.

I'm not saying it's proper or right to love a student, and I'm not going to pretend I never did anything about it, because I did, but I can say I didn't do much.

All I did was to bring the office assistant to the dance and threaten to kill her.

In the movie about George and the angel, the angel shows George what the world would be like if George had never existed. It turns out that without George the world would be a cold, dark place. Without George people would be poor and lonely. Some people would be dead because he hadn't been there to save them. Others would be older than they would be if he had lived. Without George a dark force would be in control, and the population would be suppressed and subdued by it. People would walk, bundled against the fierce winds, to their coal stoves to eat their bland Christmas dinners alone.

The moral of the movie is that, well, it's too bad that George is so unhappy and that he never got to do the things he wanted to do, that he never even got to form a clear idea of what he might *want* to do, had instead carried with him in his heart all these years a vague longing, a sense that somehow this was all wrong, that there was a shimmering ship bumping around out there in the dark that he'd wanted to board, not knowing where it was headed but feeling so trapped and helpless where he was that he had to believe the ship would bring him someplace better. It's too bad that's how it was for him, that his life had been so sad, but on the upside, look how much his misery was doing for others. His daily struggles, his failures, his defeats, somehow held in place this delicate system, so that while the population wasn't happy exactly, at least they weren't despondent or dead.

3.

It was toward the end of the semester. We were rushing toward winter break, zooming around the hallways. Outside, the city looked as if it had been tacked up and smudged with a thumb. It was the days of early darkness, a few sprigs of tinsel. No snow, but somehow we had slush or something slushish and damp on the streets.

"How would you like to go to an Indian dance?" the office assistant said to me.

"What kind of an Indian are you supposed to be?" I said.

On Saturday morning I drove to her neighborhood. It was the first clear bright day we'd had in weeks. Her neighborhood consisted of a set of small streets squeezed between two enormous bridges. She lived at one end of a long brick street that started out luminous, with shiny storefronts and upscale groceries, and smoothed out into pretty little residential three-flats, painted matte colors or made of brown stones. As I drove down it, I could see glimpses of the river between buildings. I pulled up and waited.

I had known my brother would die young and he did. I had known my neighbor would die. I had known about a high school friend and about another friend who became a lover and then went back to being a friend and then was dead.

This was the kind of neighborhood where people live long lives.

The office assistant came out of the building. She was carrying a large black case, like for a cumbersome instrument. "What is that?" I said.

"Our costumes," she said.

The dance turned out to be incredibly far. It took hours to get there. We drove on roads leading out of the city and into the vast land of America. It was a hell of a lot of highway out there unreeling beside the median strip, dry fields behind chain-link fences, antenna towers, tollbooths, flagpoles, sky. It was the kind of drive where you pass a series of billboards and road signs that promise there will be snow cones, there will be rest in forty-eight miles, God is on the way. There was a sudden insane rainstorm, clear out of a drained day. The rain drummed down so hard on the car it drowned out our voices. All we could see were stars of water on the windshield. We were driving through outer space, through a comet.

"I'm going to pull over," I said.

"No," she said. "Go."

After a while the rain dried up, and we were once again going over the empty land, passing an occasional spray of houses, the lost communities of our citizenry. A line of fat white birds flew by overhead, making it look like real work to get where they were going.

"Is the dance on a reservation?"

No, what did I think, the assistant wondered, that the reservations were just there for anyone to go in and steal out of their wigwams?

"Where, then?"

Well, I'd see, for God's sake. Now would I quit asking questions and listen to the story the assistant was trying to tell about her mother, something about the costumes, how her mother had sewed them with her own fingers based on a Native American costume description. Her mother had supported her through everything. When she drew comic books her mother had always been the first to read them. When she had love problems she could always bring them home. She'd had drug troubles, she'd suffered rejection from her father, but her mother had always been there.

I still hadn't told her that no matter how great her mother was I wasn't wearing any fucking Indian costume.

Another note about the movie. The office assistant had not been comparing me to George, the lead, who at the end of the movie cries out that he is grateful for his bad life and enjoins his daughter to get over to that piano and play them all a song. I was being compared to Mary, his wife, who, if *she* were not around, nothing would be much different—George would have married a different lady, that's all—and I have to say I do see the connection. Nothing would be different if I weren't around. I haven't caused anything, good or bad. Even if I have done something inadvertently, as, say, in the movies when a man moves a cup and a thousand years later all of humanity explodes, it's likely that if I hadn't been born, my mother would have had a different baby around the same time and that baby would have been somewhat like me or mostly like me and would have made similar choices, probably the very same ones, and she would be here right now instead of me, feeling the things that I feel in my stead. And any ill or beneficial effects that I may have caused would be caused by her, not me. She'd take care of moving or not moving any cup that I would have or not.

"You should quit that job," said the office assistant. "You're no good at it."

"I do all right," I said. "You might let me help you out with those essays."

"What essays?"

"The 99s."

"Not this again."

"Did we talk about this?"

"What makes you think you have any reason to ask me for a favor?"

"Not a favor. I'm doing you a turn. A friendly turn, friend to friend."

"You think we're friends? Why do you think I asked you along? You have a car. I asked five other people before you."

"I'll pay you a hundred dollars," I said.

This made her laugh. "You think I'm going to risk my job for a hundred bucks?"

"A thousand."

She looked over at me then, and I could see she knew I had my secret reasons for wanting to do this, reasons that were in some way shameful. And she knew it because she had her own dark, shameful secrets, all you had to do was look at her to see them, lurking behind her face, old pains, secrets having to do with the ancient beginnings of her life—with the end of it too.

"Pull over," she said.

"Fine," I said. "Let's go home."

"No way," she said. "I just have to pee."

We were on the blankest, bleakest stretch of road of the whole trip so far. I don't know why she chose that moment and not twenty minutes back at the gas station and not twenty ahead into whatever was up there waiting.

"All right, all right," I said. I eased to the side of the road. "Hurry." She got out and ran over the brown earth.

I stared out the windshield at the flat land. Bits of rain and mud were still coming down. I waited. I considered dumping the costumes on the side of the road where she wouldn't see.

The thing about the kid's music was that you didn't know what was going to happen next. You'd think you knew where it was going but you were wrong. There are very few parts of life like that.

What was she taking so long for? I stretched my neck around, saw nothing. The land around me seemed pressed into the ground, the blades of grass crushed, the few trees bent and barren. I noted the time on the dashboard. She'd been gone twenty minutes. I turned off the engine, put on the flashers. Got out. It was damn cold. Was she playing a trick on me? Had somebody picked her up out there? Was I supposed to wait here for hours and then, after dark, drive back lost, run out of gas, wander around on these roads with a gas can, which I didn't even have, only to be made fun of on Monday? I knew there was a game that went something like that, but in the version I knew, the person in the field was the one left behind. The one in the car was the one who laughed.

I called to her. I locked the car, took a few steps in the direction I thought she'd gone. It was early afternoon by this time but the sky had turned a heavy dark gray. I stepped into the field and looked back at my car to be sure she wasn't springing out, breaking a window, hot-wiring the car, and speeding away without me. The wind swayed the antenna. I walked farther into the field. It was when I came to a little block of cement, no higher than my knee, that I finally heard her.

"Hey! Hey!"

"Where are you?" I said. On the other side of the cement was a hole. I leaned in and saw her. "What are you doing in there?" I said.

It was a well that had been partially filled in. The sides were smooth. Her face was turned up to me, and in that moment her death came at me so strongly and vividly I felt dazed. "That's the stupidest question anyone has ever asked me in my life," she said. "Didn't you hear me screaming?"

The fact is, no, I hadn't, until I was almost upon her. The wind, I guess. From the road I hadn't heard a thing. The well was far too deep to climb out of. She could have been out here for days. She could have never been found.

"Are you hurt?" I called down.

"I'm wet. There's mud."

"Did you break anything?"

"I don't think so. Get help."

I hesitated. If I left, went driving down the road, I was pretty sure I'd never find her again.

"Maybe I have something in my car," I said.

"Well, go look."

I ran back to the car, studying the angle so I'd find my way back. I had so much crap in my trunk—crates of books, laundry detergents. I had a board she might be able to grab onto. I found a piece of rope from when I'd tied my mattress to the roof and moved over two blocks. I ran back to the well.

"I've got this rope," I said. "Might be long enough." I crouched down on the wet ground.

"Toss me an end."

I almost tossed her an end.

I didn't toss her an end.

I dangled the rope out of her reach. "You'll put me down?"

"Put you down?" She jumped for it, missed.

"The 99s. You'll let me read?"

"For fuck's sake," she shouted.

"Will you?" I waved the rope between us.

She thought about it. "No," she said.

"Suit yourself," I said. I pulled the rope out of sight. So it turned out her death was by my own hand, or lack of, it appeared. I walked away.

I heard her call, "You don't scare me . . ." and then her voice was gone. I went back to the car.

It may seem like I was being heroic here, trying to save this kid, but the truth is I was just grateful to be feeling something.

I started the car. If she was gone, paperwork would jam up for weeks. There'd be an administrative breakdown. Next week was finals. They'd be grateful to me for volunteering to do the essays.

"Don't worry about 99," I'd say. "I've got it covered on this end."

If, at that moment, someone had been strolling along, they would have thought I was checking my map, not leaving a life in a hole. And if someone were looking in from overhead, she, in her hole, would look completely separate from me. What was really going on was a fact she and I would share and no one else would ever know, because there was no one looking down from the clouds. Civilization settled on that a century ago. It would be her word against mine for all eternity, and who would ever believe a person would do something like that?

I shut off the car. I got out of the car and went back. "You still there?" I said.

"No, I left," she said.

I didn't ask her if she'd changed her mind, if she was ready to beg. I just lowered the rope and she grabbed it.

I had done this for a kid who'd never even looked my way. I grasped the rope with all my might and, inch by inch, I pulled her out.

Something she had on me, this assistant, which I didn't know at the time, was that I had been fired already. Or not hired back. The next semester's class assignments were sitting in our boxes. There was nothing in my box. I just hadn't realized it yet. There'd been complaints about me, poor evaluations. The students in my 99s had the lowest passing rates. For two weeks now she'd been trying to tell me and I'd ignored her. I'd thought she was just being mean.

Me? If I had been her, I would have agreed to anything. I would have let her assist in whatever she wanted if she had assisted me just then. And assuming she did lift me out, there was no way I would have still gone to the dance with a nut like that, but she was. The fact that she was capable of that, of refusing me and now of brushing off the dirt, hopping into the car, slamming the door, and saying, "We're almost there!" made me a little afraid of her.

We arrived. It was a regular grade school and the dance was held in the gym. And, yes, she had been telling the truth. Regular Native Americans were coming in and going out. And, yes, they had on their regular traditional outfits, just like she had said they would, and some of them had on a piece of a different outfit—from when the British came galloping across the land and the Native Americans knocked them over with a spear and took their jackets and then passed them from hand to hand until today, when one showed up wearing a Benjamin Franklin jacket and another showed up in a white wig, and isn't that interesting? Yes, it is.

Everyone started dancing. There were a couple of men on the side with some drums.

"Now, look," I told the office assistant, "you don't have to stick to the story. Everybody here knows that we're not Native Americans and that they all are, and what do you think they're thinking about us?"

"But I have our costumes." She patted her box.

"All right, let's see them," I said. "Let's have a look, but even in traditional Native American outfits we are not going to look like Native Americans. Nobody's going to believe it."

"But wait till they see me dance," she said.

She opened the box. Inside were two giant pom-poms, that's what they looked like. Each costume was made out of bright orange yarn, long strings of it, and it covered your whole body and even had a flap for the head. She put it on me. I stood there and let her. Then she put on her own costume. The other dancers had on animal hides, beaded dresses, but no one tried to keep her from dancing. They just stopped and stared as the assistant, in her orange outfit, walked out onto the dance floor. No one seemed able to believe what they saw. Of course, I did not dance. Then she came back and got me.

They'd had meetings about me, my name was on the table. There was no way she could have assigned me to do it. So that part I understand. But this is what I wonder: Why had she asked me to drive her to the dance? Was she that nervy? Or was it possible that she meant to warn me, give me advice?

So she got me into the costume, she had me beat on that, but the fact was: she was still going to die. Pulling her out had done nothing. I'd win in the end—not a race I was particularly excited about, a pain-in-the-ass race, one I hadn't asked to be in, one that was far lonelier than I'd expected. But she would be gone and I'd be going on. So we each had something on the other, the office assistant and I, when we went out onto that dance floor.

The kid would not die young. He would live on and on, much longer than the office assistant, much longer than I. He'd live almost forever. I know that because the next semester I had to find out if he'd passed the class and made a life in these United States, or if he'd failed, returned to his war-torn land, fought, and died. I snuck into the school several times after I'd been let go, skulked around the cafeteria looking for him. Finally one day I saw him coming out of the elevator, saw his face, and I hurried back outside.

The office assistant must have slid his paper into the "pass" pile a week before she died. She'd seen me with his file. It wouldn't have taken a genius to put it together.

Two weeks after the dance she leaped off the building, made the papers.

Okay, so what, so we look crazy in these pom-poms. Leave the poor assistant alone. Imagine what she must have been through to wind up looking like that. Imagine what her life must have been like, having a mother who would make something like these. Imagine what suffering she has had that I will never know. Just clear the floor for her. Everybody get out of the way—can't you see the office assistant wants to dance? Would you give her a little space? Give her a little music too? A little bang on the drum for her to stomp a foot to? Well, the Native Americans were ready to see something like that, so they took seats in the bleachers to watch. And as for me, I may be an old maid, and I may spend my life loving people who never loved me, and loving them in ways that aren't good for me, but I stepped around with her. I danced.

Stay Where You Are

A man in fatigues stepped out of the brush and onto the gravel. He must have come off a small path of some sort because no branches snapped when he came out. He turned and pointed a machine gun at them—maybe more like *toward* them. He called out something neither of them understood.

"Now what," said Jane. "What's this soldier want?"

Max lifted a hand in greeting. "Hullo, we're waiting for the bus," he called.

The man in fatigues walked over and said some sentences in Spanish. He kept the gun casually pointed their way. He was young. One of his boots scraped a bit on the ground.

"Maybe it's about the chairs," Jane suggested. Max had borrowed the chairs from the coffee farm off the road. She had told him not to, because there might not be time to run them back when the bus came, but Max had done it anyway.

"You can take the chairs back," Jane said to the gunman now. She stood and pointed at her chair.

The gunman didn't seem interested in the chairs. He moved the gun from side to side, explaining. He wore an army cap pulled low over his eyes.

"We're waiting for the bus," Max said. "The Tuesday bus?" He sighed. "They give these kids these weapons to go out and wave around like hands." He slapped his thighs and got to his feet. He was at least a full head taller than the gunman.

The gunman waited, listening. He spoke again, louder this time, and gestured with the gun toward the place in the trees he'd exited from.

"You want us to go with you? Take us to the station, is that it?" Max turned to Jane. "Could be there's a hurricane coming through. An evacuation?"

"Hummm," said Jane. She studied the sky for a storm. "Too bad he doesn't speak English."

Max frowned.

They'd argued the night before because she wanted to stop in the next country and take a language. Six weeks. Spanish school. Learn something. Hordes of people were doing it and it looked like fun. But Max detested school—being rooted to the ground, potted. He'd been to fifty-eight countries and never learned a language other than his own. He was no good at language. He never had a problem making himself understood. He could pantomime. "Besides, everybody speaks English these days," he'd said.

So they would accompany the gunman. But now what were they supposed to do with their packs? Max and Jane stood over the packs, deciding. The gunman waited. If they weren't going to be long, they could just leave the packs here. No one came down this road. Max and Jane had been walking up and down it for days and had seen hardly a soul. Even if someone did come along, Max didn't think they'd make off with the packs. On the other hand, Jane said, the two of them might be kept awhile at the station.

What damn luck.

The gunman interrupted them irritably.

Max and Jane looked up. "We'll probably miss the bus, you understand," Max said. "The Tuesday bus?"

They got their packs on.

The three of them entered the rain forest in the same spot the gunman had come out. Indeed it was a very small footpath, so small it could overgrow itself in days. It must have been well used despite its thinness. Max, then Jane, stepped through the trees, the gunman behind. Max and Jane walked easily, without the usual timidity of the tourist. Wet leaves hit their faces and arms. The rain forest hung in loops around them.

In fact they'd been stopped by the authorities before, many times—mostly in order to be herded back onto the tourist tracks or pumped clean of any cash they were carrying, and once in Morocco to make Jane put on more clothes (she'd been wearing a [really rather modest] bathing suit). Never been delayed more than a few hours but it would be unfortunate to miss the bus, Max thought. On the other hand, these military men might arrange a ride back to town for them, might even bring them themselves in a jeep. You never knew. Might as well make the best of it. Was Jane listening to all these species of bird?

"How close are we to the river?" Max called back to the gunman, who didn't respond. "We saw a waterfall yesterday that couldn't be beat. I say, my dear, was that a waterfall?"

"All right," she said. "Okay."

"Would you believe," Max called back to the gunman, "I have a wife who complains about being taken on a tropical vacation? Other women say, 'You never take me anywhere.'"

"Vacation?" said Jane. "Who takes a vacation for eighteen years?"

She'd been sixteen when they met, an English schoolgirl. He liked to say he stole her from her father, and it wasn't a big stretch. He'd been working on an oil rig twenty miles out on the ocean. Three-month shifts. All men. The boss, her father, had brought her on board. What sort of a dull-headed move was that, to bring your sixteen-year-old daughter out to a place like that?

Oil rig: square island, salt and steel, concrete, fish, everything the color of water.

Max had been thirty-four at the time, married, with a daughter in Sussex. He was thirty-six and divorced when he took Jane away. The first place they'd gone was Africa, where they'd stayed for years, far from anything she'd ever known, Max the only familiar object for thousands of miles, anyone else days away. It was like being the last two people on earth. It was like you yourself had sent everyone off, except for the man with you—the only man left on earth. It was like being in one of those movies about that, about you being the only ones who had ever done this, your great idea, and his. At first.

But then the movie keeps going, five years, eight years, twelve. Eventually you want a movie like that to be over, you want to see a different movie, change the channel, but it keeps going. Then one day fifteen, sixteen years in, you're suddenly sick of it—not horrified, not scared—just annoyed and sick to death of it, sick of yourself, sick of him. It's like waking up in someone else's bed and knowing just how you'd gotten there.

They'd been going like this for eighteen years, half her life, never stopping.

The gunman prodded Jane with the gun when she stopped behind Max. "Ow," she said. "Max, he just stabbed me with that monstrous weapon!"

The gunman said something angrily in Spanish.

"Hey, watch where you direct that thing, kiddo," Max said, and moved Jane, rubbing her elbow, around him. "You go ahead of me."

They all continued walking.

Of course they stop, Max would counter. They ran out of money every few years. Remember she'd been a postal lady in New Zealand? Carried sacks of mail. And she'd swabbed decks on a ship like a man, all the way across the Indian Ocean. Hardy girl, always had been. One of the first things he'd liked about her.

And how about the time they became citizens of New Zealand? he'd say. You have to hold still for an honor like that. Nobody just throws citizenship papers into the airplane after you. Remember they got to meet the president on New Year's Day? They got to shake hands with the president.

His favorite defense. How about the time in New Zealand?

Yes, but they left the next day! The *very day* after they received their citizenship, they left, Jane would say. And now they didn't own anything other than the belongings in their packs and it might be nice to.

Didn't own! Max would say. They still had some carpets in New Zealand, remember? They'd gotten them in India and brought them along, left them with the neighbors in Wellington. They could go back and get those carpets anytime they liked. Is that what she wanted? Carpets?

She didn't want carpets.

Citizens of New Zealand, he'd say. Hands in pants. Looking around. As a matter of fact, this is a nice spot. Maybe they could be citizens here too.

They were deep in the rain forest now, dense damp foliage, vines like arms crossing in front of them, sun blocked by a canopy of leaf-knotted trees meters overhead. Bugs whipped past them, loud as motors, biting their hands and getting caught in their sweaty hair, sticking to an eye. Jane brushed them aside.

God, she hated this now. She could almost imagine another story for herself but she had no faith in it. No faith in herself. She couldn't really imagine what that other story might be. It had been seven years since she'd seen her father. Nine since she'd seen her sister. Imagine going nine years without seeing your sister.

Max thought she didn't even like her family. He certainly didn't. But why not invite them out if she missed them so much? Meet up in Peru for some hiking. Like his daughter had done that one time. That had been good fun.

Was he referring to the time his daughter met them in Africa and got so sick she nearly died, and so afraid she flew home halfway through the trip? The time his own daughter had to fly six thousand miles and risk death to see her dad?

She used to not like her family.

Yes, well, she used to be a teenager.

The three of them rounded a corner, stepped into a clearing, a gathering of huts. "Ah, here we are," said Max. He stopped and surveyed the patch of border trees, the tents propped between the clotheslines, the overturned crates. "Not much of a station. What is this, an outpost camp?"

The three walkers rounded the corner, stepped into the clearing. The gunman looked around and stopped.

He was thinking (in Spanish): Where the fuck did they go? Fuck.

He kept his gun trained on the Americans.

The bus comes on Tuesday, Max thought. All the people at the coffee farm had told them that. Mimed it. Mimed Tuesday.

Jane was thinking: Shit.

The gunman was thinking: Shit. They'd gone off without him, the bastards. What, they'd woken up, seen he was gone, and left? Or, worse, had they not even noticed he was gone and just marched off without him? And here he'd been so crafty, bringing back two Americans, surprise, surprise! Now who's the champion? But no one was here.

He took out his cell phone.

He told the Americans to shut up.

And another thing was America. The argument always went like this: Max despised first-world countries, but Jane wanted to go. Might be fun to ride a tandem bike across America. Picnic basket on the back.

Oh no, Max always said. They'd been to America once already and they weren't going back. America had been exactly as they'd expected, exactly as they'd always heard. First thing that happens, they buy a cup of tea and the lady says, "Have a nice day!" Just like an American on the television. He and Jane got on a bus and a fight broke out between a young man and the driver. The two of them screaming at each other until the man got off the bus, cursing. Violent country. He's surprised they didn't get killed.

Jane: They spent one day in America on their way to Mexico. Nineteen hours.

Max: And it was just as they thought it'd be. No reason to go back.

Jane: Besides, this was America. They were in America now. America was this whole thing, up and down.

Jane thought, Shit. That is, she was thinking about shit. She couldn't see a camp like this one—strung canvas, fire pit, encroaching foliage—without the image coming into her mind of a camp they'd stayed in at the edge of the Sahara. The latrine had filled to the top and then run over. People had to stand on the seat to shit into the pile. Soon the latrine was so full of shit, you just shat near it. It became a sort of "latrine area," and you tried to get your shit in the vicinity of it on the ground there without getting too close yourself and stepping in it and tracking it back into the camp. Then, of course, the rains came and drained all that shit right into the camp. It all came floating in, getting into everything. The tents, the mosquito nets, the clotheslines. It got onto hands and smeared into hair.

The gunman now very decidedly had the gun pointed at them, which was unfriendly, for one, and dangerous, but Max and Jane were both determined not to make a thing of it. It wasn't as though they'd never had a gun pointed at them before, and to complain like an American usually made things worse.

"He's asking to see our passports," Max said. "Here you go, then."

The gunman took the passports. He noted they were not blue and didn't want to think about that. He put them in his pocket and paced. His boot scraped. Too big. He almost tripped. He'd been given a fucking mismatched set of shoes. He told the Americans to stop looking at him and go sit by the pit. He had to make some calls.

The gunman said something in Spanish. Max and Jane didn't understand, but they understood the waving gun and went where the gunman said.

Yes, they'd been captured before. In the late nineties, by a tribe. In order to pass through certain territories you had to ask permission of the head of the tribe. Usually it was no trouble. But one time a tribe took the opportunity to lock them up. Jane had been certain it was the end. But Max had charmed them all, chattered away in English—which none of them understood. The tribe leader had offered Max a dark mixture, the kind of thing that could kill a man not used to it, but Max had drunk it down and asked for more, and by the end of the night they were all singing songs.

They squatted in the dirt with their packs on. A line of ants was re-forming itself around them. The gunman poked at the tents with the gun, making agitated sounds into his cell phone.

Jane slapped the bugs. The ground was burned moss and forest and soot. The sun was coming on full by now, breaking into the clearing. Sweat was coming down their faces and arms. They took off their packs.

The gunman came back over to them with something else in his hand.

The gunman was thinking they had to be at the main camp by now. Were they not answering on purpose? He didn't have a second piece of rope, but in his experience, Americans were an obedient bunch, as long as you had a gun. They'd just stare, or weep—though they always talked, you couldn't shut them up. He couldn't herd two Americans fourteen kilometers, he knew. When were those assholes coming back?

Yes, Max could talk all day to people who didn't understand him, but with tourists who spoke English, he just shut up. He let her take over, had never been much for small talk. He'd nod out on the stair or watch the light play on the plaza tile through the trees—who knew what he was thinking—while she talked to the tourists about wristwatches that stopped in the tropical air, places to use the bathroom. All travelers love to talk about shit and bugs. He didn't need anyone but her.

Last month in Nicaragua they'd met two sisters who had been too scared of getting robbed to do anything but hide in their room, mosquito nets lowered around them. Max and Jane had brought the sisters along with them for a few days, showed them the ropes. They'd been in awe of Max—in the old way. (People used to be so impressed with Max.) Last fun he and Jane had had.

What she herself had been in awe of at one time, she couldn't quite reach anymore when she looked at him. She'd been thinking for two years now about leaving him.

But what was left for him without her? Middle age giving way to old age and the difficulties of that, disenfranchised family, cemented-in views that were now outdated, no friends, no money, no hobbies that one could do while sitting still, no abilities of any kind other than not speaking fifty-eight languages, a keen knack for spotting animals no one else could see in the trees, a knack for drinking the locals' water anywhere in the world (this last was no cheap trick: you had to be determined, unafraid of illness or death, although in most places consuming water wasn't considered a special skill, you don't get a paycheck for being thirsty).

All either of them had was this thing they'd created, this twoness between them. If she left (or made *him* leave, rather— there could be no question of her walking off and leaving him somewhere, unimaginable, he, the walking man) what was left for him?

Did he think about that? What did he think about? All these years with him and she still didn't know.

For Jane, sure, there might be enough. She was still young enough to create more for herself, to make it someplace, find someone. An adequate life, a job in retail, maybe, or being a company rep or an exec or something. Maybe she'd find that life exotic after the one she'd led. Or nicely quaint. So far she hadn't done it because of what it could become in the long run— what they'd always feared, what they'd always been running from, the drab, the dull, the dumb, and then death. She'd always said she could never go in for a regular job, house, kids, vacation a few weeks a year. Avoidance of this had been their mainstay, their mythology. But now this option seemed inviting compared to what Max would become by himself, alone, aging. Might as well be dead.

So that's how Jane thought of him, and Max, in a place deep inside himself, knew it. And knew, too, that she might be right. But he also knew it didn't matter, for he had already done the one great thing he would do (not travel all over the world, anyone could do that—didn't even need the resources, just the desire): he'd loved this one woman for eighteen years.

The gunman held the piece of rope in his hands. He put down his gun and began to forcibly tie Max's hands together behind him.

"Now, is this really necessary, mate?"

Jane looked on, uncertain. All right, no, they'd never had their hands tied before, but that didn't mean they should get excited, right? She couldn't stop him somehow, could she? How? Grab the gun? "I wonder if this is a stitch-up," Jane said.

Max was nodding. "They've mistook us for foreign intruders. These fellows are trained to think that anyone near the mountains is trying to take over their government."

"I don't wonder with your shave," she said. "We look like riffraff."

They were sitting facing each other by the fire pit. The gunman was sulking by the clotheslines with his phone. Jane was parched.

"You know," Max said, "I don't think this is a military man. I believe what we have here is an insurgent. A rebel of some kind."

They both looked at the gunman.

"I'm sure I'm right about this," he said. "Look at the uniform. It's not a proper military uniform. The top and bottom don't match."

"That doesn't mean anything. Who can tell who wears what?" Jane said.

Max considered. "What war do they have going on here? Do they have one?"

"I thought it was over ages ago."

"Insurrections, maybe? Mountain revolts?"

"Well, if we read the papers," said Jane, smartly. "If we spoke Spanish." She couldn't resist.

"Hey," Max called to the gunman, "are you a revolutionary or a soldier? We can't tell."

The gunman didn't know he was being spoken to.

"Some new revolution, perhaps," Max said, looking back from the gunman.

"No doubt," Jane said. One they hadn't heard of, since they didn't read the papers, since they didn't speak the language, since they didn't care what was going on around them other than what they could see before them. Only way to know a country is just to be in it, he'd always said. Walk the land. Be among the people. The political stuff was so boring. It changed every month.

"This is the dullest thing that's ever happened to us," she said.

"Get off," Max said. They'd been through worse, Max thought. This wasn't going to be something they always talked about. Besides, what was this—a situation? Were they being kidnapped? If so, Max wondered whom this guy thought they were going to call for money. No one in *Max's* family was going to donate to the cause. And these revolutionaries or whoever they were better have a man who spoke a little English, because if you thought *Max* was bad at languages, he doubted his family believed other languages *existed*.

Things had been better in Africa, Max was thinking. Things had been better in New Zealand. Only the Americas. The Americas got them all right. Every time.

"Cállate," the gunman called to the American, who blinked at him and stopped talking for a moment but then went on talking. The gunman went over and punched the American in the face and came back.

As for the gunman, we may wonder who he was and where he came from. He was much like a regular gunman for the insurgents: He'd been born not ten kilometers from this spot and loved it here, despite the rain, the poverty, the fighting. He'd grown up doing gunman activities and wanting to do them. He'd learned how to shoot at age nine (he was now nineteen), he knew people who'd died by bullet, he'd shot people he hadn't known, he loved the cool nights of the dry season, he'd had his share of fistfights and knife fights and preferred fists because knives were too psychological and fistfights ended fast. He believed in no land tariffs. He believed in school for kids (he himself had gone three years). He'd buried his mother and two brothers.

He was different from a regular gunman in that he'd been to the States once, had hated it, and had not wanted to stay. He preferred to stay here, where he had the hope of one day being a leader, though he knew that those who knew him would say there was little chance of that. He lacked charisma, they would say. And maybe he was different in that he didn't hate all Americans, though he wished those two over there weren't there.

One other fact about the gunman: he'd never loved. He wasn't a psychopath or anything so ugly as that. He'd had women (and once a man) but he couldn't say he'd ever felt love, and he understood this was strange, since the men he knew were always loving their heads off all over the place. He just felt dry. He had desire and lust but never longing, and this bothered him.

But it was only a fact about him, not a defining characteristic, one short fact among others—another being that he could fall from anywhere and not hurt himself, had been like that since he was a kid, could fall out of trees, off roofs. He was known for it, had earned nicknames.

What was that sound? That faint roar in the distance? Was that the bus?

Jane looked over at Max. He'd heard it too. But what were they going to do about it?

The gunman listened for his men but heard only the Wednesday bus, a day early this week apparently.

As for Max, he'd already done the great thing he would do.

They were quiet, all of them, contemplating the glassy future. "Look," said Max at last. "There's going to be a moment when you can get away. I want you to take that moment and do something with it."

"What am I supposed to do with it?"

"Get away."

"How? Where? What about you?"

"Don't sit there asking questions like that when the moment comes, all right?"

Jane was thinking: See? He had a plan. If this fellow with his gun thought a piece of string would hold Max back, well, he had another think coming. There wasn't a knot Max couldn't untie. It was as if he'd been a sailor. And Max had vision. He knew how to see monkeys in the trees. When no one else could see anything but green, Max would spot dozens.

Max was brave, had always been brave. She knew that. He had talents. A punch in the face was nothing to him. She'd seen him stand still when the gorillas came after you. *That* was brave. They had gone to the gorilla preserve in Tanzania some years back, the one people make films about. The gorilla experts, they say to you, "Okay, listen up, folks. This is what's going to happen. The gorillas are going to come after you. They'll make a big noise and throw dirt and run right at you. It's what they do, the gorillas. It's a test. You have to just wait it out. When they charge, don't move—stay where you are." They tell you that and you repeat it in your mind, *Stay where you are, stay where you are,* but then when this five-hundred-pound gorilla charges at you, you just throw up your hands and run screaming. Supposedly it takes months to learn how not to. Only way to make friends with the fellows, the guides said.

Max was the one who hadn't run. Even the professionals—the newer ones, anyway—ran. The scientists ran, but Max didn't. Jane had been amazed. Everyone had been.

Maybe she'd go back to England, see her sister. Maybe she'd go back to New Zealand, where she had friends. She wouldn't go back to Africa, though things had been better there.

Jane looked up and realized Max had scooted to his feet, hands still behind him, so fast she hadn't heard him. The gunman strode over shouting and Max shouted back. The gunman raised the gun to his face. Jane was screaming. But she got up and ran screaming into the forest (didn't sit there asking questions) because what else was she supposed to do? He'd told her to do that and if he had told her to, it meant that this was his plan for her and so he had a plan for himself, too—which was what? That he get punched in the face again? That he get shot? That he get himself killed? That he not care about himself as long as she got away? What kind of a plan was that? She realized she was still screaming so she stopped. Then she heard a shot and started screaming again.

He would one day love. By the time he got around to it, this day with the two Americans would have been long ago (two years) and so much would have taken place in the meantime (he'd leave the insurgents, move to the city with his uncle) that he wouldn't even think of them anymore, except when he had to use his right arm (constantly), because that's where the American (Brit, actually, and New Zealander, but the gunman would never know that) had shot him, and the place still ached after all this time. The American had brought out his hands, untied, and grabbed the gun with a grip the gunman never would have expected— not so hard that he couldn't have wrenched it away—he was trained for this sort of thing, after all, had killed a man in four minutes with his hands. But the problem was the shoe. It was too big, his foot slid in it, and at the very moment he needed to have a good grip on the ground he couldn't get it, and the American toppled him over and shot him in the arm and then stood over him, staring like a fucking American, gun hanging at his side. The last thing the gunman saw, before the blood made him lower his head, was the two of them turning away, running, the woman pulling the man's arm.

Later, that image, the two of them in that instant, would come into his mind again and again, but it would no longer be there when he finally did love, because his own image, his own love, came back at him instead. But the Americans (New Zealanders, rather) stayed in his mind for longer than most things.

You would have thought that going through that would keep them together, and it did for a while, but humans go through all sorts of episodes, and it doesn't always settle their hearts.

At the end of it all, after she'd left—well, after he left (because she made him) and, not knowing what she was doing, she left too—and after they both found themselves in countries far away from each other, in places that didn't have the energy or beauty the two of them had once found in such places together (although there is nothing unique in that, the world dims over time—though maybe it wouldn't have had the evil tint that it eventually seemed to Max to have, or the lifeless, meaningless tint that it seemed to Jane to have, if they hadn't parted ways)—after all that, each of them installed on separate continents, she wrote a letter to no one of significance: one of the sisters they'd met in Nicaragua with whom they'd traveled for a few days. Jane wrote to explain, felt she had to explain to this stranger why she'd left him (or made him leave, the walking man) and what it had felt like.

It was like leaving him in the clearing with the gunman. That's how it felt. Like she'd been given a chance to get away, and he hadn't. He'd given her a chance and she'd taken it, knowing where she was leaving him and in what condition, knowing the fear and loneliness he must have felt, but she'd done it, run on a bed of leaves and needles, under a canopy of trees (didn't ask questions)—or that had been the plan, though it hadn't turned out that way.

At first she was running. She realized she was still screaming and she closed her mouth. She heard the shot and started screaming again. She was moving away, running through a jungle made of roots and water and bugs, the sun coming through the branches.

Then she slowed, then stopped. She didn't move, thinking.

She turned and went back.

She could see a break in the trees and was moving toward it. Should she go in there? She didn't know who had been shot—Max or the gunman. She was pushing away the branches, she was pushing herself through, and then she stepped out to greet him (*I came back for you*) or to be shot.

2

To the Ocean

At the desk they said they encouraged guests not to walk, but she was determined. She took the useless map and they set out, she and her husband, following the boardwalk. When the boardwalk ended, they followed the path, she saying the whole way, "Of course we can walk. Why don't they want us to walk!" until the path ended and they stepped out onto a field, which she determined was a golf course. They hiked across that—"Bourgeois assholes," she was saying, marching along, swinging her arms. Her husband kept saying, "Oh, here's where it ends," and "I don't think we're allowed in there," and "I'm not walking in that," while she thought, If I had married someone else, it wouldn't be like this. She thought longingly of a man she might have married, blurry, nondescript, one who no doubt would be laughing and running up the hills. This, while her sister sent a text: *Where are you? We took the shuttle. We've been here half an hour.*

Later, at the picnic, her husband would describe it to the sister, who'd be laughing. "Oh, I can see it!" the sister would say. "I can see her coming down the side of the mountain, struggling through the trees, bruised and bleeding." "There she goes!" her husband would say about her imaginary figure cutting through the brush. And the sister and husband would both continue to tease her throughout the day, provide running commentary on her actions. "Making sandwiches for the revolution," they'd say. "Pouring coffee for the revolution. Having a swim for the revolution." When they clearly didn't understand her at all.

Before all that, while they were still on their way, she and her husband came to the edge of the golf course and looked out over the cliffs and beyond, the first glimpse of their destination—the water, hazy and distant. There was so much to get through between here and there: trees, a whole forest of them, the downside of a steep mountain, tall grasses, weeds to your hips, misunderstandings, ticks and mosquitoes and spiders and other disappointments, lost jobs, lost faculties, dying parents, and so much more. "Don't," he said, but she would do it. She steadied herself to walk in.

The Vice President of Pretzels

Now, I've been eating the pretzels with my wife since we met in 1962 and I don't think they are especially good. I certainly don't think they are "thicker," but she had been eating them far longer than I, and she insisted the formula had changed, or perhaps the machinery, and that as a result they were very slightly "thicker," and she would no longer eat them and complained about them for months. She tried to call the manufacturer but got only recorded voice greetings. She wrote emails and even letters but nobody answered. My wife is not one to give up on a thing and I'd be hearing about it until I died. So one day I was looking at the package, while she complained behind me, and I said, "By God, we should drive to the factory and tell them in person." We are retired now and have an RV. According to the package, the factory was only two states away.

We drove sixteen hours, camped at the Walmart overnight, and in the morning we arrived at the factory, far off the highway in the middle of long rectangles of fields. We parked our RV in the lot and went up to the front desk. My wife tried to explain at reception but the woman behind the desk had a look on her face and was obviously not impressed. I thought we'd have to leave, head home without having achieved our objective, but then a man in a suit walked in the front door and stopped. "I can't help but overhear," he said. "I'm the vice president of the company. What seems to be the trouble?"

My wife began her story again. God help me, I love this woman but I could see on the face of the vice president of pretzels that he was not understanding and was on the verge of backing away into the inner offices.

I touched his shoulder. "This woman," I said expansively and gestured toward my wife, "is your oldest customer. She has been eating your pretzels since she was four years old. That's sixty-seven years. And she says the pretzels have changed. We have come all this way from Arizona to tell you."

And my wife had him do the taste test. She went out to the RV and retrieved the pretzels—the new kind and the old kind, she had saved a bag of the old to demonstrate the difference to people. He tried them both and looked thoughtful. He admitted that, yes, the pretzels were slightly thicker but he insisted the pretzel formula had not changed and the pretzel manufacturing equipment had not changed. He wondered whether my wife might like some of their new peanut butter pretzels or caramel pretzels, free of charge, and we took them because I like them but my wife was not interested. She wanted only the thinner pretzels. He said if we left our address, he would look into the matter and report back once he was able to determine what had happened. We drove home. After that the vice president of pretzels continued to send pretzels. Every few months he sent another box of butter pretzels or chocolate pretzels and a bigger box on holidays with a card that read, *For our oldest customer*. I'd say, "Look at these delicious chocolate pretzels," and she'd say, "Eat them yourself," and I'd say, "The vice president sent them, just for you," and she'd say, "Those places are overrun with vice presidents." After a few years he stopped sending them.

Defects

He is making a list of his defects, he says. He is using a new system to manage his total quality. "Total quality of what?" she says. "Of life," he says. In this case, his life. It could be other things, too, like a business, but in this case it is his life and his improving the total quality of it by eliminating his defeats.

Defects.

Yes, that's what he meant to say. Defects, the things he does that compromise his total quality. For example, each time he eats too much, he makes a little mark here. And each time he sees someone he could network with and does not take the opportunity, he makes a little mark there.

What happens if he gets too many defections?

Too many defects and his life is compromised, he says. Then he says, Maybe she could make a list of defects too. Then they would be doing an activity together, which she has often said they don't do. And she says she doesn't have any defects, but perhaps she could do benefits. For example, every time she does something good, she could get a mark. That isn't how this is done, he says. And anyway he likes it this way. And anyway she does have defects. "Such as what?" she says. Such as being late. "That's not a defect," she says.

And he says, It doesn't compromise her total quality of life, being late all the time and making everyone wait? No, she says. She doesn't mind being late. But maybe, she says, it compromises *his* total quality because he has to wait for her and that drives him crazy so perhaps she could make it his defect: every time she is late, he gets a mark. That's another one of her defects, he says, negative attitude. She could keep track of them for him, she offers.

A Crossroads

They come to it every day: eight lanes across, a bewildering system of lights overhead, a tangle of arrows painted along the ground, signs of various sizes posted around with additional directives for the motorist. Every day they wait for the lights to cycle through, the traffic to inch forward, their dashboard clocks marking what has been wasted on this dispiriting square of cement. They can't be blamed if they are quick to honk and rev their engines.

They are aware that these sounds—their motors and horns— might be heard by the businesses on the four corners, the food mart, the fast food, the dry cleaner. The air itself is so cluttered with wires and posts, drivers may miss the small ranch house on the fourth corner, wedged into the lot before the strip mall begins, a house made of the cheapest beige siding, with large awnings over the windows so that the interior must be dark. When they do spot it from their cars, they think of the unhappy family who lives there.

But in fact the family is not unhappy, a single working mother with two small children. The mother cannot believe her luck, after all she's been through. Her own house at last, its spacious rooms, modern appliances, its standing in an upstanding suburb where her children are carried to school by bus for free. How those new windows slide closed with a smooth thwack! Even a small backyard for them all to sit on a summer afternoon, the younger child in a kiddie pool, the girl in the grass, the mother with a bowl of pretzels on her stomach (where a deadly cancer grows). If only the woman's mother could see her now, how proud she'd be.

An Opera Season

1. *Tosca* by Giacomo Puccini
Tosca is so jealous that she stirs up trouble for her boyfriend. He and his comrades wind up jailed, tortured, shot, dead. She, too, is soon dead, tossing herself off a roof. The highlight: the chief of police takes off his shirt and walks around on the stage in a circle. Others come on and join him, but do not remove their shirts. People outside die one at a time.

2. *The Barber of Seville* by Gioachino Rossini
He's a man-about-town. He dresses up in costumes. He pretends to be first poor, then drunk, then sober. He breaks in through the window and sings. His reasons are strange but simple, and he sings about them. The woman he loves figures none of it out until he explains it to her very carefully over and over. Finally she understands and sings about it. Everyone sings about it. They all take turns singing about it, and then they all sing together about it.

3. *Jenůfa* by Leoš Janáček
In this opera, all the characters are relations. Jenůfa is related to all the men, and the men are all related to each other, and the

mother is a relation in two ways—as a stepmother and in the usual biological way.

Jenůfa doesn't end up with the one she loved forever in act one, but with the one who, about halfway through, stabbed her in the face. Neither one wants to marry Jenůfa. She isn't likable, for one. She has a stabbed face. And now an awkward baby.

4. *Rigoletto* by Giuseppe Verdi

A father does not wish his daughter to receive visitors, and the boys are off their heads about it.

5. *Aida* by Giuseppe Verdi

The pharaoh's daughter loves a man who doesn't love her. This is the story: how he doesn't love her back and how she loves him anyway.

She's entirely nice. Anyone would love her—she's pretty, she's got money—but other events make it impossible: natural disaster, parental privilege, another woman, war. But she shows a little steadiness, a little loyalty. Even when the man doesn't want her, she just goes on wanting him.

Finally she has him buried alive. That's the point—you want the thing you can't have and you don't get it, so you kill it. Meanwhile some other people run around, clutter up the stage. No one knows who they are or why they won't shut up. They sing about their business. The gossips. The reprobates. Get them out of here.

6. *Susannah* by Carlisle Floyd

Susannah is kicked out of the church and her fiancé is unfaithful. Men from the military step out, do a ballet dance. There is foreboding. There is noise in the distance. Women shriek and the enemy dies.

7. *Alcina* by George Frideric Handel

Performed by only women this time. There were enough male singers but we decided to let the women play all the parts. Some of the women are supposed to be men, and others are supposed to be women dressed as men for duplicitous purposes involving love. With so many women, the opera is about five hours long. The women fall in love with each other over and over. They enter and exit, always in love and singing about it. One woman who is dressed as a man wants to be with another woman who is dressed as a man. But the second woman wants to be with a third. This is act one. In act two, the matches disintegrate and recombine into new configurations.

The end? The singers stagger onto the stage, one by one confessing what they once were: neither men nor wiomen. *I was a rock, I a tree, I a wave in the ocean . . .*

How to Dispel Your Illusions

•

First you need to not know what you want. This can go on for years—and for many of us it already has and you may be past this step—so that when you finally do settle on an ambition of some sort you are so grateful to feel desire that you want to hold on to it at all costs, and the thought of heading back to that earlier, more hopeless space is enough to drive you forward.

Be sure the ambition is lofty—why would you settle? And then strive for it. Say, for example, your goal is to be a writer. Set all sorts of mini-goals along the way and celebrate each post as you pass, though use it only to propel you on to the next one. At first the posts are fairly easy to pass and you run by them with glee, but before long the years are going by and the posts seem farther apart, take much longer to get to, and, in fact, there's just a random splattering of them out there, not in a line, maybe some of them hidden or not on your plane of field at all but on some other plane you can't get to, and you are sick of trying. After all, what is the point?

More years pass and you are wandering the desert alone, picking up rocks, your guide is lost or was never there, your gratitude for feeling desire is waning. What is so great about wanting when what you want is so elusive and in any case why did you want it to begin with? You forget what it was like to not know what you want, and you find yourself drifting back to that space again, although you have come so far out, have passed so many posts that you don't know where you are now, have no courage to go back and take another direction entirely—why should you if this is what it comes to? Besides, you are so old and tired.

It was nice to have once wanted, you think (though you were fooled), maybe you could just sit down in a grassy field (if you can find one out here, unlikely, maybe some gravel) and reflect on what a fine job you once did, and look up at the sky. Were they illusions? You hadn't thought so. You could have sworn they were more rugged than that. But it turned out not to be so. A few heavy rains washed them away. A few earthquakes came along and swallowed them.

Granted

Two historians received a grant to go to a certain country. They had to spend all of the money inside the country, have itemized receipts (a credit card slip alone did not count), and they couldn't come home until they did. They paid for their plane tickets, their rent-a-car. They bought their travel apps, their phrase book and recordings, but that wasn't nearly enough. They had drinks on the plane, a meal at the airport. But there were still thousands to spend, and the hotels in the country were so cheap and there were no restaurants. Even the bologna sandwiches the hotel lady made them (because at last they were hungry) were free. The two historians tried to spend it all, really, but it was impossible. They walked through the town, holding out their pesos—"someone, please, take these"—while the citizens looked on, confused. The two historians drove through the mountains but each town held less: no gas stations, no shops, no hotels. They slept under the stars in the breeze. Finally, when the car broke down and their bodies were thin skeletons and the sun was low in the sky, they picked up their satchels and wandered into the hills. *"Un recibo por favor, por favor."* That was the last night they were seen.

My Daughter Debbie

She doesn't have any skills. While she was growing up, I always encouraged her to learn how to do something. I told her she should become an X-ray technician. Then she would always have work and she could pursue her hobbies on the weekend. She did philosophy in college and I said she could be an X-ray technician and still read her philosophy books and have a good paycheck and a skill she could move around with, because she likes to move. I never saw anyone move so much. Then that gave me the idea that she could be a flight attendant. She could travel and get paid for it and still read her philosophy books. By this time she was doing graduate classes in philosophy, and I told her not to come looking to me or her father for a handout. She needed to have a job with a paycheck, I said, and—see this?—she dropped out of the graduate classes, wasted all that time and money.

Years went by and she seemed to be doing nothing.

I told her she should be a social worker, like I was, because she loves people and is so good with them, especially men. One night, when she was four years old, we had a handsome man over for dinner, friend of her father's from school, and she came walking down the stairs like a movie star and said, "Who is *that?*" A little flirt. She's still like that, always has a boyfriend. Never had much of an interest in children—which she will regret one day, as I always tell her and as her grandmother does too. A woman without children will never be fulfilled. But she does seem to get a lot of boyfriends who are all entirely inappropriate, too old for her, brooding, and you can't understand what they do for a living, can't understand a word of what they write in magazines or say on the radio, and she always leaves them, every time, she's always packing up and moving out, cannot make a commitment.

She had a strange brother, that's why she likes these strange men.

So she decided not to go on with the philosophy (one smart choice) and then she did nothing (but was too busy to answer the phone) and then she had that bad breakup with a strange man we all thought she'd marry but frankly were grateful she did not. Then she moved in with a woman who I'm sure was unbalanced (I don't know what was going on there) and I pleaded with her to get therapy.

"Now, look," I said. "There are perfectly good, well-trained therapists. There is some discount therapy downtown and they are very selective about who they'll take. You are ideal for it."

They took her right away.

She quit going, of course, and wouldn't say why, so who knows. Then I helped her get a perfectly good job. I flew out to see her. I went through the want ads for her because she wouldn't leave the apartment. I uploaded her résumé for her because she wouldn't get out of bed. Finally she got a job—not a lot of money but at least a job—at a lead-detection clinic, but after a few months, she quit, just walked out one day. Then she quit another job she had after that, I don't even remember what that one was, at a homeless shelter. Then she had another at a day camp. And another as a secretary for the rabbi. She just kept quitting. It was sad. We all said so. "She just quits everything she does," we said. "Remember piano," we said. "Remember ballet." Then she met some entirely inappropriate man and I heard nothing from her for months and then her phone was disconnected.

The next thing we knew she was calling herself a writer.

Now somehow she has managed to get this good job—I don't know how, I don't know how she does anything, but she did, and we all breathed a sigh of relief because we were thinking, It is just sad how Debbie turned out, it is just really sad, with all her potential, she was such a beautiful child and now look at her. That's what we were saying, my sister especially (well, we'll just see how *hers* turn out). Now we're all holding our breath. First we were all holding our breath because honestly I wasn't sure if she was telling the truth, you never can tell with her. Then her sister found her name on the school website and we all sighed with relief.

Then we were saying, "Will she stay at the job?" Because sometimes she just runs off. And she seemed to stay. Now we're saying, "Will they fire her?" Because she can't get a book published, a real one, with a real publisher, not a publisher no one's ever heard of with a weird name, and that's why I always ask her about it. I tell her, "Look, you are not moving back in with me and your father for us to support you, so you can forget it. You better just write that book." If she's a writer, like she says, why won't she write it? Either she's a writer or she isn't, I tell her. And she better say she's a writer because otherwise, well, the job is out. Her first real job, I might add.

We went to visit her a few months ago, her father and I. She wouldn't do one thing that I asked and wouldn't tell me anything either. First I asked her did she know she was throwing money in the toilet, just flushing it down, and she said, No, she did not know that. I said, "So what do you think paying rent is?" Perfectly good houses standing all around her and she rents the worst one in town. Then I asked her, "How is that book coming along? Because if you don't write one, aren't you going to lose your job?"

The fact is I know something about jobs. I was a social worker from the time Debbie was a year old until her sister was born—then I had to stop because I had three little ones at home. But I was good at being a social worker. I helped young girls who had problems. The girls I helped liked me and gave me gifts like candles and cards. After I left, one missed me and came by the house. I always planned to go back. But then we moved for my husband's job and I needed a new certificate for the state and then my mother was sick and I had to fly back and forth. Now, well, I've got my alumni club and book group. No one wants to hire someone my age.

My daughter Debbie is a writer and it is such a relief to have her *be* something, because she was always something to me. She was my favorite, secretly, dancing around the house. She drew me pictures, sang about her dolls. I used to use her name as my password at work. She was just a tiny thing—so was I back then, I was a child when I married, a child when I had her—and she was happy, not this silent sullen mop she is now. Somehow she got away from me. I don't know how it happened. She's the one I know the least.

Once, when she was very small, she decided to run away. I don't remember what it was about but there she was. She had her toy suitcase and she was taking a few slices of cheese from the fridge. I said to her, "Where are you going?" And she said, "I'm running away." She was sniffly and furious. I did not laugh. I said to her, "Why do you want to do that?" And she said, "Because Dad's mean." So it must have been something her father did. Her sister was always her father's friend and Debbie was mine. I used to tell her jokes and read her books. She used to play fairy tale under my desk. I do like to encourage her.

I said to her, "I'd like it if you would stay."

Open Water

By the next time she saw him, she had discovered, without much effort and without him knowing, his last name, then his entire work history, previous places of residence, former wife's occupation and location, children's names, and she had seen photos of friends of them all. She had learned about his preferences, his dreams, that he believed in a benevolent God, that he enjoyed the open water of a calm lake and the challenge of a narrow rapid. These facts in hand, she had projected into the future what she might say to impress him. She imagined being at his lonely bachelor pad in his four-story apartment complex (she had studied pictures of the fountains and two pools at the complex, the weight room, the bike storage, knew his probable rent depending on whether he had two or three bedrooms—or had he opted for only one?). She imagined his voice getting gruffer as he told her his story (she knew he'd met his wife in college and had married young, just two years after they'd finished their degrees—maybe they'd grown apart, maybe she'd left him, felt she'd given him and their children her best years, willingly, but now wanted more, and why not?). She imagined him telling her all this in his kitchen, the new appliances, the island with its bar stools, going over the facts she already knew. She saw his eyes on her slim body, imagined him pulling her close (he had attended the university where she now taught, and one of his sons was headed there now, the son who looked so much like him, same blue eyes, same thin neck, same tousled hair, a boy who'd won the eco-science fair that year, beat out fifty-four other projects, according to the Web announcement, was going places, this boy). She had already imagined it all, so much so that when she finally did see him, she felt unable to speak. Two short years back he'd had an awakening sweep over him, or a disaster befall him— she wasn't sure which. He'd left his place of employment after twelve years with the company, where he'd been such a presence, had been featured among the top executives in the country, not that long ago. But something had gone wrong: he'd divorced, made a move and it didn't seem lateral, though maybe it was, she really had no idea what any of it meant, the ridiculous job titles and descriptions that all sounded the same, vague and grandiose but also somewhat small in their ambitions.

He'd been through so much. They'd been through it, in a way, together, and now what was left? They were long past pleasantries. If there was anywhere to go from here, it would be in silent understanding, the two of them on the shore of the lake he weekly boated, or alone in one of his quiet rooms. But did she love him? Was he enough? Was she ready to disrupt the course of her life, become a stepmother to two teenagers, for this man, a man who loved water, who'd had children too young and now found himself at one end of a long corridor, more alone than he thought he'd be, but ready for better: this man, cheerful, smiling nonchalantly? She wondered this when he arrived and she watched him across the room, talking to some of the others.

Alas, she already had the sick feeling of an ending inside her, the long sorrow of a slow breakup, of the impatience with which she would await his emails if he didn't write, her boredom with his boys (who played basketball and water-skied), their dislike of her and her efforts to assuage it—for what? For this blue-eyed man? She was so disappointed, in this, in them, had wanted much, was offering all, though he had asked for so little. Still she was willing to try.

The Applicant

We chose his application because the writing was good but also because the poor man lived in a foreign land where he'd been placed in a camp for no reason other than the religion of his fore-fathers, and had wasted away there for eight long years, during which time he tried to better himself in whatever way he could, amid atrocities and so on, only to emerge with a deeper empa-thy for all humankind and begin writing stories of his trials and the trials of the men and women who'd stood around him in the yard, sat next to him by the wall, the ones who'd disappeared, the ones who'd been beaten with padlocks. We spoke on his behalf with increasing eloquence to the higher administration, because of the cost of bringing him on a visa, until we were all imagining him attending our program and afterward going on to write *important work* that could *transform* the world, and how our program would be responsible. We won over the administra-tion and secured his passage.

But after he arrived in the fall amid internal departmental fanfare we had to admit he was not writing about the camp. His stories didn't include a word about it, because in fact he did not want to transform anybody, and he did not want to write stories anymore that presented his damaged life and the lives of the men and women he once knew. He was hoping to leave that behind at last, start new—could you blame him?—write about sailing away on an ocean, and when that wasn't far enough, shooting away from the earth in a spaceship, and when that wasn't far enough, heading out of the solar system toward distant stars.

The Walk

The idea was to go for a walk: the baby in a stroller, the child by the hand, the path straight and scenic, the weather warm and breezy, the family fine and in good humor.

But the dog got too hot and lay panting on the ground, and they'd forgotten again to bring the water. The baby (Kryptonite, they called her) was in one of her moods, weeping on and off, refusing to sit in the stroller, tugging off her hat and throwing it into the dirt, so that they had to stop every few yards, retrieve the hat, pass the baby from one parent to the other because she wanted only to be with the father while he, exhausted ("weakened," he said), kept handing her back.

The father didn't want to carry the baby. He'd carried the baby yesterday when they'd gone to see the sand dunes. Kryptonite had wailed and was hot and had put a fistful of sand into her mouth, and they'd forgotten the water in the car then too. He had sat down in the sand for a while, calling, "We are not having another kid," a sentence he'd been repeating the whole trip (he no longer called it a vacation), often within earshot of the mother, who, to his horror, only laughed.

Kryptonite always wanted the father, the mother was thinking. Both the children did, even though without the mother they'd be dead in a day. Kryptonite could hog a whole event, anytime,

anywhere. The mother couldn't manage to have a simple conversation with the father without an elaborate pause in the road to
hand off baby, transfer bags, retrieve hat, and so on, couldn't manage to have a simple joke between them like they used to. "Daddy's
girl," the mother kept saying each time the baby reached for
him—sweetly at first, but after a while with clenched teeth. The
baby went back and forth, screaming, between them.

The father was hot, like the dog, who kept dropping to the
ground. The father worried about the dog. He felt every emotion
the dog did—powerfully—felt at least as much pain as the dog
did at any moment, felt the dog's hunger, felt the dog's thirst.
Felt the dog's loneliness and isolation at being the only one of its
kind amid this crowd, felt the suffering of walking a path in the
heat wearing a heavy fur coat, of walking with no destination,
no food or water, tied to a rope, dragged like a slave.

The mother could tell just what the father was thinking. He
didn't have to say a word. Just the way he moved his feet along
the ground said it all, the mother thought for the tenth time
that day.

The older child was the only one among them who was having any fun. She was on her feet, too old for any stroller. She was
so used to her younger sister's cries that she didn't hear them
("a Kryptonite shield," the father always said, a talent that later
in life would be seen as a defect—"lack of empathy," people
would say), so used to her parents bickering that she didn't hear
them either, uninterested in the suffering dog. She strolled down
the path looking at flowers.

Online

The plan is to cut back in half-hour increments until she is down to two hours per day. She is old enough to have a memory of life off-line, but it fades each year and now seems far away. She doesn't recall what she did with that time and whether it was fulfilling.

The first week is so easy, she doesn't feel it. She can be online twenty-three and a half hours a day! Weeks go by, months, and she doesn't notice how severely she is restricting her use. Four months pass—a restriction of eight hours—and still she is fine as long as she doesn't wake in the night and in a fit of insomnia browse. Besides, one must sometimes look up from the screen, if only to pay for a soda, or walk down the hall. Six months in, she hits the twelve-hour mark and that's when the pain sets in. She leaves her phone at home and now she can't walk down the street and check her mail. She goes to the movies but she can't look at the screen while looking at the screen. More hours open up, hours that must be filled with activities, and she can't remember what there is to do in the world other than study screens of various sizes with various intentions. Now she treasures each minute she has, and her time off-line feels ghostly, like time spent waiting for her real time, her life time, her online time.

What am I doing out here? she thinks. What is the point?

Out of sheer boredom she reads a magazine. She has trouble concentrating and at first can think of nothing but how bored she is, but then she smiles in a couple of places and learns one interesting fact (sea seals, like parrots, can mimic!) that she tells a friend over lunch, a friend she made plans with because she is so bored. Now she is down to six hours a day online and she really is at a loss. She exercises every day. She calls her family to chat. (Why do people have families if they're so boring to talk to?) She does a little home improvement. She sits at the window for minutes at a time. She thinks she could learn an instrument, become a famous star? Or maybe she'll help the world in some way, give? That's a smug thought, but she thinks it anyway, since she has nothing else to do. The time lowers to three hours a day online, and she casts desperate looks at people on the streets and in shops, and she thinks, How do people fill their days? Are they unhappy, having to face their own brains so often and with such constancy?

Is it worth it, this dull life? She feels—as she switches off the light, going to sleep early since there is nothing else to do—that she can glimpse in the distance a time when she might enjoy an experience for what it is, when she might read a book and want to read it, when she might take a walk and find it fun, when she might hear a joke and laugh without awareness of her loss. It is with that hope that she does this, for its possibility.

Your Character

Your character is wounded in a ditch. Your character is stuck in lockdown. Your character stalls out in a long line of traffic. Your character meets the last man on earth. Your character stays by the body, waits for the police to arrive.

Your character runs away from home.

An unnamed man arrives on the scene.

Your character gets pushed into a fountain. Your character walks home in the rain. Your character is lost outside in the middle of a storm. Your character cries in a bathroom stall. Your character leaps from a sinking boat.

Your character makes a snowman.

Insert random song-and-dance act. Insert random talking animal.

Every plot has room for an assassin or two.

Your character convinces the public to try out a new body-modification unit that starts out innocent, then gets mildly addicting, and then becomes a physiological need. By the end the body is converted into a plastic-like substance.

Your character is shunned by all but one (a talking duck).

Your character blows up the love interest—an accident, but still.

Your character beds an old man. Your character sleeps on a board beneath a bridge. Your character stays up all night, cries all night, wakes in the night, walks in the moonlight, sleeptalks. Your character lies down in the graveyard. Your character wakes six weeks later to learn most of the ship's crew is dead.

Your character just isn't sure true love exists.

Your character is arrested—it's a wrong place, wrong time scenario. Your character vaults from the roof. Your character stands up and screams. Your character collapses on the sidewalk. Your character takes the ashes, runs through the funeral. Your character feels the water closing overhead.

A pre-dystopic government is in power.

Pirates attack!

The sidekick is lost. The sidekick has the wrong briefcase. The technology fails. The sidekick, who was sitting on a desert island, raggedy, starving, alone, fading, suddenly drops out of the sky and onto your character.

The love interest is too small to survive. The love interest falls in love with someone else, quits the quest. Might return later. The love interest has been cursed and lost his memory. Does not remember your character. The love interest prays in an ancient temple. The love interest avoids your character at the school dance.

Your character just wants a normal life—but that is the only thing under heaven that your character cannot have.

Your character dies. The story goes on without her. The water is rising, the sky is breaking, the air is filling with poison. The bottom of the window is six feet up.

Fear of Trees

He hadn't seen a tree in ten years. There were no trees in any of the four prisons he'd lived in and he moved from prison to prison in a windowless van in chains. When he arrived home at last, the trees on his street were so tall that he was afraid and kept ducking. They seemed about to fall over. They would crash into the houses, crush the cars, kill his family, lay waste to civilization.

3

Voltaire Night

I'm the one who started it. I was depressed as hell and wanted to share my bad news. "Has anyone read *Candide*?" I said. I don't even recall what the bad news was now but it must have had to do with a certain man who didn't love me anymore. In those days I felt most of the time like someone had knocked me in the head with a brick, and even though I had stopped drinking, I had started again, and the way I saw it, a real brick in the head would have been okay because then I'd be dead or at least unconscious.

I had a job teaching a class in the adult-ed program of a fancy prestigious college. The class went one winter night a week, and while the school was fancy, the adult-ed program was not—classes were not held on the beautiful medieval campus, but shoved over into a hideous office building downtown in order for the working citizens of our land to have easier access to higher learning, though we all knew the truth: it was to keep the fake teachers and students from mingling with (and possibly infecting) the real ones. The hallways of the downtown building were lined with artful black-and-white photographs of the real campus so that we could all look at the place we'd been denied. The classrooms in the downtown building did not have windows. This was an architectural feat, maybe even a masterpiece, something in the league of M. C. Escher, because the outside of the building had windows running up and down three sides and while, yes, one side had no windows, it was not the side that held our classrooms. I sometimes stood at the foot of the building, looking up and marveling at how this had been accomplished.

Still, getting the job was my one obvious piece of luck that year. The pay wasn't great, but it was decent and it beat the other adjunct work I was doing. I was teaching all over town and could barely pay the rent. I was drinking in the cheapest bars, driving home blind.

The people who took these adult-ed classes tended to be smart, overeducated for jobs that were no longer fulfilling or that had never satisfied in the first place—journalists, lawyers—and now, in their middle years, they recalled that they had once wanted something artistic for their lives but it had not worked out, and despite whatever trappings they had—spouses, houses, tykes—they found themselves confronting a deep, colorless meaninglessness each day. They thought that maybe realizing their early dreams would change all that. They wrote books six thousand pages long and made jokes about bringing them to class in a dump truck. Or they wrote nothing but had a great idea for a story that they recorded on their phones and had their assistants transcribe. Or their spouses were working, and they themselves had quit their numbing jobs, were staying home to write, give it a go at last. Their writing—let's be honest—was nothing to shout about. Not good, mostly unreadable. No control or sense of timing, no grasp of narrative beyond cliché. But often the language itself had personality, and a clear voice came through: sardonic, witty, self-deprecating, with a tarp of sad earnestness over it, all of which I liked, so I found it easy to read the pages they gave me and to encourage them.

In Voltaire's *Candide*, there's a certain passage where a huge crowd wants to board a boat, all vying for the same seat that Candide—luckless man, but in this one instance he is lucky and in possession of some extra cash—has offered to pay for. The seat will go, he says, to the man or woman most bad off among them. One by one they choose their woes and tell their tales. That scene—communal, classroom-like, someone in charge judging their stories and making promises no one could keep—and these students, with me as their leader, reminded me of that.

After the final class of my first course at the school, the students suggested we go for a drink.

I didn't usually go for drinks with my students. I knew teachers who did and I found it unprofessional and revolting, though that would not have stopped me. Neither would the fact that I had sworn to quit drinking. But the school had put in place a policy that applied even to the dubious adult ed. I'd had to sign a statement. Still, an end-of-term drink seemed like a nice idea.

We walked four blocks through the freezing cold to an upscale, unpopular joint in the nighttime-deadtime downtown. We sat in giant stuffed chairs in a dark room, empty of anyone but us and the bartender. They all looked over at me, waiting. At last I said, "Has anyone read *Candide*?"

"Yes, yes," they murmured. "Voltaire. Of course." As I said, this was an educated crowd. They'd read it in college, they said. Or they'd read it when they were twelve and had found it confusing. Or they'd liked it and had read his other works since and found them less fun.

"Let's play a game," I said. "Let's each tell the story of the worst thing that's happened to us."

"In our lives?"

I hesitated. I wanted to talk about the boyfriend who'd left me, and even in my traumatized state I had to admit it wasn't the worst thing that had happened in my life. I'd had people die on me. I'd once had a fire burn up all my things. Besides, this boyfriend left me a lot. We were on the third or the fourth time now, depending on how you were counting. Those were the days when the same boyfriend left me over and over, and each time felt like a tragedy.

"Lately," I said.

They looked hesitant.

"And whoever tells the worst story wins," I said.

"What do they win?"

"Well, they get to be the winner."

They looked disappointed. "But the winner of what?"

"Voltaire night," I said.

As a matter of fact, Candide had solicited his crowd, had not wanted to sail alone, and I could understand that. He'd had it announced in town, had taken out an ad in a circular: *Will pay passage for the most unfortunate man in the land.* So many unfortunate men showed up, an entire fleet of boats could not have taken them all away.

The students were into it, but nervous. The first told a silly story, something about a drawer that held important papers getting stuck and his having to saw it open with a chain saw. Another said she'd gained ten pounds. Another said her final grandparent had died and she was unnerved—what, with only one generation between her and death. A second round of drinks and the stories grew more personal. One man divorced last month. He hadn't wanted a divorce. He was in a new apartment in a strange neighborhood. He'd been married fourteen years. He felt so old. One man's teenager had run away that year and it had taken a week to find her, and when he did finally locate her and went to pick her up, the girl screamed, "I hate you!" while he stood in the driveway, stunned. Why did she hate him? What had he done? One woman had learned she had cancer. She'd had her first round of radiation last week—a curable kind, but still. The mood in the room grew somber, and we felt protective of one another, commiserative, full of solidarity. Then one guy said, "Well, I got a flat last week in the rain," and we all shouted, "You lose!" and threw pretzels and straws at him.

I did tell the story of the boyfriend, not the long absurd version that my friends were all sick of, but the miniature version, the kind I'd tell on the bus, and I told it in a dramatic fashion: "The man I love no longer loves me and I can't seem to get over him, no matter what I do or where I go." The students all rose to my defense. They were indignant, outraged. The guy was obviously a fool. I deserved better. "I know, I know," I said, shaking my head. Who can explain love? we all wondered, eating our peanut mix. Who can explain the recession of love? Love's sneaky decline?

I don't recall who won Voltaire night that first time, but I know we voted and had a winner who received extra rounds of commiseration and drinks and a couple of comradely hugs as we all parted at the door and hurried through the cold for separate trains or lots.

It was a grand night, our first Voltaire night.

The class went six weeks and restarted the next month like a new moon. Perhaps because I'd done well with the first class, or perhaps because no one in the office was paying any attention at all, I was given the course again and several students from the first class signed up. It was an open class, noncredit, at the service of anyone in the world who could show up on Tuesdays and pay the (exorbitant) fee. But the old students claimed an elevated status over the new ones anyway—not by their superior writing (they were all equally bad and no one had improved) but by talking about Voltaire night. The best night of the class, they agreed. One of the best nights of the past year, in fact, for them all. It had been so fun. And enriching. Too bad the new students had missed out.

Hey, the new students said, *they* wanted a chance at Voltaire night. It wasn't fair that I had picked favorites and wouldn't grant the new students this educational opportunity. So we planned a second Voltaire night, and the final night of the class, we trudged out into the cold.

It was March now, but the wind was still punishing in that evil Chicago way. I talked again about the cruel boyfriend who didn't love me, who even after these months was still causing me pain. He had come back in the meantime but had left again, and again I got all the commiseration I could hope for, and Voltaire night was special all over again—even if we did stay out a bit late, due to the fact that the bar closed at one, and maybe we had too many drinks, but it was okay. We all waved good-bye at last and crept off into the night calling that we'd see one another next month.

It didn't slip by me that the meaninglessness on their faces might gleam only when they came to class—those faces turned toward me, hoping for not success, but proof that they were at least *worthy* of some intangible (maybe nonexistent) thing, even if they never got it. But maybe at home they were happy. A few, of course, took the class merely as an extracurricular, nothing more—women, mostly. These had happy lives that brought fulfillment. They tended to take the class for only one session, wrote friendly, honest evaluations encouraging me to do such and such (what that thing was always differed: talk more, talk less, fewer or more handouts), and they'd wave good-bye and we'd never see them again. Some were like that, but not many.

Voltaire night took hold. It became an institution, part of class. Leading up to it, the students conferred. Where should it be held? Should food be involved? And the parameters—the worst thing in the past five years? since Christmas? as a kid? They'd settle in and tell their stories as if we were around a campfire, as if these were the stories of their lives: their disappointments and frustrations, what they'd striven for and hadn't gotten, the promises made to them that had been broken, the people who were gone or who were still there but seemed changed somehow, not what they'd once been, or perhaps it was the students themselves who had changed. Blame the vicissitudes of life, or, alternately, its flatness, the dullness of it, the sad fact of aging. This of course took a lot longer than our original three-minute summaries, so Voltaire night grew long. We'd all be drunk, having closed down several places, and the folks from the suburbs missed the very last train and had to curl on a bench at the station, like criminals down on their luck (which weren't we all, in some way?), until the 5:30 a.m. shuttle. But it was worth it, we all said, for how else could everyone have gotten a turn? How else could everyone have told their story?

As for me, I'd arrive home at four in the morning and spend a few days cursing myself. The trouble I could get in for this. Unseemly. Voltaire night was out of control, a monster I had to rein in but didn't know how to rein in. I didn't want to rein it in. Voltaire night was the one night I looked forward to, all of that sitting around feeling sorry for ourselves. I would have liked to do it every night.

There was the Voltaire night when Max accidently smashed

several glasses onto the floor and Stuart threw up on the sidewalk. There was the Voltaire night I somehow found myself separated from them all at two in the morning, smoking pot with strangers at a faraway club. How had I gotten there?

There were other things going on with me. Voltaire night was just a handful of nights out of that year, but the other nights weren't so very different.

I had to change. In many ways I had to change.

One Voltaire night, a clear spring night, after a winter that had seemed to go on for years (and in fact this was my second year on the job), the students voted to tell the worst thing of their entire lives.

I don't know why we hadn't done that yet. Worst thing ever. It seems like it would be a fast place to go once you're on the worst-thing roller coaster, but we hadn't. Maybe we'd refrained because we knew once we'd done it, future Voltaire nights would be uncomfortable. Once you'd told the worst, how could you complain about the past three months, which contained only the usual disillusionments, the familiar slow-burn panic that you were doing nothing with your life, had not lived up to your "potential," or, worse, you had and it had changed nothing, that you had not yet even learned how to love? But the students voted. The worst-ever Voltaire night. We went to a nice place for dinner and ordered several bottles of wine.

Among us was a new guy who had been with us only one session and had barely spoken in class. I hadn't noticed him much among the brash, flirty, loud men. He raised his glass. "I'll go next."

"All right, all right," we said. The newcomers often went first, were fool enough to go when people were just settling in. The regulars knew to wait. The best spot was an hour or two in, when people were happy, when the deep-level drunk hadn't set in yet, turning the night into a disco or a disorderly blur.

"The worst thing that ever happened to me," he said, "began with an experiment. You ever see those ads asking for human subjects? A hundred bucks to take some drugs, fifty to do some puzzles?"

"Uh-huh," we said, meeting eyes with one another. A human-subject-experiment story, here we go. Our stories would top that.

"I was living in Hyde Park, newly married. My wife was pregnant. Four months. We were overjoyed, but poor. I did freelance design back then, my wife was in sales, and no matter how much work I managed to scrape together, it wasn't going to be enough. So I used to answer those ads for a few bucks. Cover an eye and identify colors. Recite words I was told to remember."

"Uh-huh," we said.

"Well, one day I came across an ad that said, *Twelve-week experiment, fifteen thousand dollars,* and I thought, Wow, fifteen thousand dollars! I went down and signed up."

I'm not sure I have the details right. I want to be clear about that. I'm not sure if it was fifteen thousand or ten or eleven, or if she was five months along or four. I'm pretty sure it was twelve weeks. What one hears at Voltaire night stays at Voltaire night, and it is only now that I am violating this contract.

"It turned out they paid you fifteen thousand dollars because the study was miserable, and no one would do it unless for a lot. They wanted to chart the temperatures of nocturnal humans—humans who had been deprived of all natural light." He leaned forward and sketched the light in the air. "So two guys came over and spent all afternoon removing the light from our apartment.

They blocked up our windows. They used heavy black boards and put black tape around the edges so no light could possibly slip in. You were required to sleep in the day and be up at night. And you were forbidden to leave the house while the least bit of sun stood in the sky."

"For twelve weeks?" we said. We were laughing hysterically.

"They gave you a sun calendar so you would know when the day was over, and since the study went into summer, you could see on the calendar that by the end you were going to be inside a lot."

"That's crazy," we said.

"You don't get used to it," he said, "if you're wondering. But that wasn't the worst part."

"What could be worse?"

"In order to have your temperature charted, you had to have a tiny rectal thermometer inserted in your anus, twenty-four hours a day for twelve weeks."

We looked around nervously to be sure we were still laughing. How much would you have to be paid to do that? we wondered. Would you do that for fifteen or eight or eleven or whatever thousand dollars? What was that worth?

"The thermometer was sort of surgically put in there. I had to go get it checked twice a week, make sure it was still in place, because a man has to shit, you know. So I'd lie in bed all day, unable to sleep, in an apartment with blackened windows, not a single slip of light, and my wife would go to work. Long after dark I'd go to the lab and bend over so they could check my thermometer. How do you feel? they'd say. Are you experiencing discomfort? Then I'd go home through the dark to the apartment and eat and watch TV and try to stay awake and do my freelance projects, although it was hard to work under those conditions and gradually I sought fewer and fewer. But still I was not unhappy, because my wife was getting a little bigger each day, a little rounder, and she held my daughter inside her (by this time we knew we had a girl), and I knew that when my daughter arrived, she would have everything she needed because of my suffering through this."

"The weeks went by and I have to admit it got worse. Outside, spring was shifting to summer, and inside, the nights grew shorter and stuffier. I stayed inside through it all. The thermometer was uncomfortable. I could feel it in there, although they'd initially told me I wouldn't. It began to get a tiny bit painful but they checked it and said it was fine. I sat up through the night, but sleeping in the day became harder as my initial determination wore off and was replaced by a lethargy. The weeks were interminable, each week seemed like an ordeal, a string of hot days before me that seemed endless. We had no air-conditioning, just a meek fan that rotated the dead air in a room whose windows were taped shut. I didn't want to spend money on an air conditioner. I barely saw my wife. She worked all day and had to be up early. She was leaving for work as I was going to sleep, though I couldn't sleep. I was achy, exhausted, although all I did was sit around, all day and night, alone mostly. Even my outings to the lab—the cooling darkness, going through the neighborhoods, outings that should have held joy because each one marked another step toward the end—were tinged with bad feelings. You'd think I'd go for walks at night, meet friends for late dinners and drinks—that's what I had planned—but I did so less and less. The thermometer was uncomfortable, I was too sleep-deprived to be much company. No, my visits to the lab, my late-night trips to the grocery, my stops for gas, became my only outings. I stayed in, watched TV or played video games that involved blowing up objects and leaving huge craters in the earth."

"Why didn't you just quit?" we said. We were not laughing. "I would have quit, by God. No way could I do that."

"That's what my wife said," he admitted. "Oh, I wanted to, all right. I came close to giving up, but if I did, all the weeks I'd suffered would be for nothing. If you quit in the middle, you got only five hundred bucks. And the truth that I hadn't told my wife was that despite my plan to double our money, I'd stopped working nearly altogether. She believed my workday began in earnest after she'd gone to sleep, but I quit the moment I saw the light switch off in the bedroom. Unless I finished the experiment and got the money, we'd wind up with a loss."

"Oh, that's bad, that's very bad," we said, settling back down.

"So the weeks stretched in front of me, and every week that passed, I thought, Thank God that's over, but the idea of six or seven more like it seemed impossible. But I thought of my coming daughter, how beautiful she'd be, how much like her mother, and I soldiered on. And one day it was five weeks left, and one day it was four weeks left, and one day it was three weeks left."

"Sometimes I just couldn't face the hot apartment and my wife, who was more annoyed by the day with the experiment. Sometimes I stopped at a bar on my way back from the lab. The first time one drink was enough to push me home. The second time it was two drinks, the third time, four. I arrived home later and later, and my wife went from annoyed to disturbed to enraged. One night (I'd gone out every other night for a week at that point), she screamed over her belly, I don't even know who you are anymore!

"I remember it so well. It felt so unfair. I was close, less than a week away, only a few more days. I screamed something back, incoherent and nasty.

"Would you just get out? she yelled. Get out, just get out.

"I'd never been a drinker, beyond some nights in college, and the bar I went to was the worst place on the planet: Christmas lights strung in July, broken tables, stained linoleum, a line of human subjects sipping their lot, the kind of place the postmen went before they shot themselves in the heart. I sat down and ordered a drink."

This was going to turn out to be the final Voltaire night, though we didn't know it yet. The restaurant was quiet that evening, glasses emptying and refilling, the windows covered in lights.

Candide and his hapless crew. I could see them in my mind, gathering on the dock, their trunks and boxes piled on the wet wood, their fingers in their pockets wrapped around their last coins, while Candide strolled among them. Why did they all want to get on that ship? What was wrong with where they were? Were they fleeing the scene? Making a humble retreat? Or had they been told—politely but firmly—to leave?

Or were they going toward something, looking for a better life?

"The next thing I remember is that I couldn't open my eyes. Something was pressing down on my face. I couldn't get the lids up. I struggled to lift myself to consciousness, felt my body pushing itself to the surface, breaking through ice and pebbles and glass. I opened my eyes.

"Illumination. Beautiful, glorious daylight. Unfettered. Lawless. It was as if a drain had been unclogged and light had spilled out—pale, glowing, garish. The earth was swept with it and yet light itself is landless, has more in common with water, the way it rushes through and fills up any space between objects.

"So this, I thought, is what it is to be nocturnal."

"Where were you?" we said. We could hardly breathe.

"That's what I was thinking. I was confused. Had I completed the experiment? Or even better, had it all been a horrible dream? Had I never attempted any experiment? Had no experiment ever existed? I tried to sit up and sleep slid off me.

"I was in my car. I had not finished the experiment. I had stayed out all night. Day was pouring over me like poisoned tar. I had no idea where I was. I felt sick in every possible way. The car wouldn't start and I was like, Fuck! I had to get out of that daylight.

"I left the car and my hangover hit me like a baseball bat. I staggered around, put my head on the hood."

"Had you been in a crash?" we said.

"I had run out of gas," he said, spreading his hands in astonishment. "I was on the emptiest road I'd ever seen. Beyond city, beyond suburbs, beyond what lay beyond suburbs—fields and summer and sky. I must have driven until the car stopped, I must have been on my way out of town—had had it, quit, left, but only gotten this far. And here it was, a perfect day. I hated myself. I began to walk."

"They had emphasized how important the final week was, how the first month was basically control. The second month showed the shift, but this final week—when the body had fully adjusted (though you never do get used to it)—was what we were all there for, the *data* (though if they knew what was going to happen, what did they bother with it for?), all for some obscure paper in some obscure journal, one experiment amid so many experiments going on all over the country, all over the world, and not just experiments, but *lives*, men and women and animals, in a vast experiment that in a thousand years will have been wiped from the earth nearly a thousand years ago. I walked two miles in the blazing sun to a gas station. Out front I stood by a sign-post and threw up in the road.

"My daughter, my wife—I'd let them down in so many ways. I'd kept my own wife in the literal dark during the most trying months of her pregnancy, had ignored her, had done no free-lance work, and now on top of that might have lost even the fif-teen grand and would sink us into debt. I paid for gas and a ride back, drove home, and crawled into bed—my wife was already gone, didn't answer my texts. I lay in bed, not sleeping.

"Hours later I got out of bed, found my phone. I had a text from her: *I've gone to stay with my sister.* I went over to the sink. I was leaning over it, wanting to vomit, and my head lifted. I found I was looking at the calendar. I'd been x-ing off the days, but I'd stopped these last couple weeks, hadn't managed even that. The final day of the experiment was circled in red. I looked at the date. I looked at my phone. I had been so distraught that I hadn't realized: the dates matched. That day, that night, was the end of the experiment. Shaking, starving, still hungover, terri-fied and tired as hell, I took a shower as it got dark. I drove to the lab."

Here's a question: How can you quantify how much a man suf-fers? How can you measure the amount of pain he has against the amount of other things he has—maybe not happiness but, at least, hope? In order to make a proper calculation, Candide would have had to know the other details of the men's lives, their weaning and rearing, first loves, last, nutrient intake, and so on. He would have needed a measuring system and ledger. It would have taken more than one night.

"I was waiting for them to come get me at the lab when my wife's sister sent me a text: *She's gone into labor.*

"*Two months early?* I texted back.

"*Seven weeks,* she texted. *We're headed for the hospital.*

"Take this thermometer out! I yelled down the hallway. We're having a baby! So at last, after all those weeks, they took it out and my butt relaxed.

"Congratulations, they said.

"Where's my check?

"We just look at the final numbers, they said. The check should arrive in three days.

"I ran to my car, praying I was on my way from the worst time in my life to the best."

"In the car my butt began spasming. They'd said it might. They'd said that when a thermometer is removed after having been there for twelve weeks, that one 'might experience some discomfort in the anal area.' This was not discomfort. This was horrible pain. Under normal circumstances I would have taken three sleeping pills and gotten into bed and not gotten up for two days. Under normal circumstances I might have gone to the hospital for myself. I was sleep-deprived, too, don't forget, and hungover. I was dizzy and sick, bursts of black and red in front of my eyes, but my wife was having our baby! I arrived at the hospital and ran in. She's coming, was all my wife said and she was smiling. I kissed her face with terror and relief.

"Her labor was long. Twenty-six hours, and I was with her, spasming the whole time. We were both exhausted. The doctor was saying we'd go one more hour and then give up and have a caesarean, but then all at once the baby was coming. The baby is coming, the baby is coming, I said. This is it, the nurses said. I held my wife's hand while she pushed and screamed. The doctor reached and—I was at my wife's head, I couldn't see. We were waiting for them to raise our beautiful squalling daughter, put an end to our misery. But the doctor didn't raise our daughter.

"Holy mother of God, said a nurse, and pulled her hands to her chest. Our Lord Jesus Christ.

"What? we said. What is it?

"I was too scared to let go of my wife's hand and walk over there. What's wrong? cried my wife, but they bundled the baby up and raced off with her, turning in the doorway to say something along the lines of We'll be right back."

I didn't know this yet, but by the time of the last Voltaire night, things were beginning to take a slow turn for the better for me. A very low creak was sounding in the wheel, but it was turning. I was managing to publish some stories at last. The horrible man was gone for good. It would be the beginning of a better life for me, though it did not feel better yet and it would take me a couple of years to roll my way out. Still a long road to happiness, but I was seeing tiny points of light in the distance and I was heading toward them. I'd teach one more class after this one at that school, but my heart wasn't in it and I didn't do a very good job. The following year I got a tenure-track position at a large university, a job I'd really wanted, and then I was gone.

"My wife and I were stunned. I ran into the hallway, but the doctor and nurses were gone. I heard my wife calling and I ran back. A nurse was there, sewing her up. She wouldn't say a word. Someone will come talk to you, she said. Just stay calm.

"What's happening? Is she alive? we said.

"Yes, she's alive, said the nurse, or at least she was.

"Was? we screamed.

"I'm sure she's still alive. Please wait. Just stay calm."

Years later this man wrote and asked me to write him a letter of recommendation, and I agreed. In the letter I wrote about Voltaire night, how it came about, how we did it for all those months, and how the night he told his story—I didn't tell the story itself—was the best Voltaire night ever, how after that we didn't even mention Voltaire night again. He had clearly won.

Years after that I heard he was dying of stomach cancer. I heard another in the group died of a brain tumor. I don't know what became of the others, though I can see them in my mind and I can imagine the joy of success rising out of them and gathering around their heads. I hope it for them. Now and then one writes a quick note to me at my university address: *Do you remember me?* I answer, *Yes, yes, I do.* They don't write again, as if they'd just needed that slim reassurance that somebody still knew what had once gone so wrong.

"Neither of us had slept in so long. It had always been night. We were both in outlandish pain. We held each other's hands and wept.

"The doctor came back. Without the baby. Where is she, we said.

"Now, stay calm, he said, using his hands to demonstrate calm.

"Quit telling us to stay calm, we said.

"Your daughter has an extremely rare muscular condition. Impossible to detect without amniocentesis.

"What? we said. What kind of condition? Will she live? Is she okay?

"She's alive but she has no muscle. Her muscle has degenerated. She is unable to sustain muscle.

"What does that mean? we said. We don't know what that means! Where is our baby? We want to see her.

"Her appearance is startling. I don't want you to be alarmed.

"We won't be alarmed, we said. Bring her, bring her.

"Okay, I'm going to bring her in for a few minutes but then we have to get her to the ICU. He paused. I need to tell you. She's going to need a lot of treatment. This condition is associated with severe disabilities, physical and mental.

"Okay, we said.

"And a short life span.

"We won't be alarmed. We promise. Bring her.

"He went out for a moment and came back. A nurse came in with a bundle and put her in my wife's arms."

At this point he pulled out his phone and held it up for us to see. "Seven years old now," he said proudly. "They said she wouldn't live three years." I took it from him. I had never seen anything like it. It was hard to know exactly how to look at her for a moment. Her face didn't look quite like a face but then I found her eyes and assembled the rest of the face around them. We all looked at the photo and then at him.

"Did you get the money?" one of us said.

But who could win the Voltaire-night prize—which was nothing, just another path over water? Which was to live your life after Voltaire night, to keep going, strike out for more, after the terrible thing had happened to you, more terrible than what had happened to anyone else, and that might turn out to be the best?

"The nurse placed the tiny bundle in my wife's arms," he said, "and I pulled back the blanket. I touched the top of her head with my hands. She was so small and her bones were visible all over her face. I could barely breathe. My God, I said, she's beautiful.

"Isn't she? said my wife. She's perfect."

Mr. Simmons Takes a Prisoner

Mr. Simmons was not a family man.

This, although he had a family. A wife, two daughters. A large apartment to put them in. A dog. He felt attached to them (fuzzy-headed, waving from a distance) as he did to certain household kinks: the sticky lock, weak showerhead. Comfortable inconveniences, he might say. He preferred the empty office on Sundays to the fussy kitchen at home. He didn't heft a pine up the steps at Christmas, perform science experiments with lightbulbs and tinfoil, romp off to the corner store for snacks. No bike rack on the Toyota, no ski trips, no corn in the City of Chicago community garden. He worked late, told the kids to cut the racket at dinner, read political magazines before bed. He sighed heavily, slammed the refrigerator door when the kids asked for cash or keys. But Mr. Simmons wasn't cruel. He never beat his family or tossed them down the stairs.

The Simmons' younger daughter entered college and the apartment grew quiet. He kept to his routine. His wife went out and got a teaching certificate, to his surprise, and within a year had a classroom of ten-year-olds. Each morning she left earlier than he, left him to rinse his cereal bowl alone. In her absence he walked through rooms spread out and white, felt the air around him, poked his head in the abandoned bathroom by the kids' rooms—

folded towels, wrapped soap, clean tiles. He thought irritably, Why do we need such a big apartment?

This was the first thing. Then, new emotions. His wife spoke endlessly on the phone to the girls, left Mr. Simmons to wait his turn to talk, helpless, dying as he stood there. Finger-drumming, wild hand signals to no avail. But when she finally handed him the phone, he found he didn't have much to say.

Or when his elder daughter announced she was moving to San Francisco with her husband, he was stunned.

"You're leaving with that truck driver?"

"He's an environmental lawyer."

"I've never seen him fit a tie around that thick neck," he said.

Minor outbursts like these increased. The family backed off in bewilderment, then ignored him.

The day after his daughter moved, he woke, put his feet in his slippers, and went looking for the dog. A bit old now, the pooch. "Here boy," he called, patted his leg, whistled. The dog limped over. "Treat? Treat?" he said. In the kitchen, he fed it a puppy biscuit, tossed it the squeaky toy. He waved from the door as he left for work. "Good boy. Sit."

That night he carried the dog into the bedroom.

"Thought the old mutt may as well stay with us tonight," he said.

"Won't your allergies bother you?" his wife asked, looking over her book.

"Allergies?"

"Your allergies, you know," she said. "Allergies."

"Oh yes." He put the dog down and shooed it into the hall.

Should he have an affair? He knew plenty of women. A proper jacket, one hand pressed to the small of her back, the other lifted to summon a taxi, her dress spinning in a slow circle. But most of the women he knew were his wife's friends—painted cracked lips, puffed hair. They had stopped talking to him beyond the required niceties years before.

He watched the women at his office. They strolled through the hallways, studied the bulletin board in the lunchroom. He pretended to be busy with the coffeemaker. He couldn't approach.

His younger daughter arrived for a visit. He followed her from room to room, knocked on her door when she shut it.

"What do they have you reading at school?" he asked, leaning in through the door.

She sat on the floor, held the dog's face with both hands and cocked it back and forth. "Nothing you'd be interested in," she said.

"What makes you think I'm not interested?" he said. "I'm not an interesting enough person to be interested? Who's paying for this education, I'd like to know?" He turned on his heel. "I expect a list by supper time!"

Later, in bed, he explained the matter to his wife in a diplomatic tone. "It doesn't matter what she reads. She has her life, I have mine. As it should be."

"Then don't make such a fuss next time," his wife said and snapped out the light.

In the lunchroom, a notice tacked to the board read like a personal message: *Illinois Prisoner Reform Association.* An ink drawing of a man in a studious pose over a book. Mr. Simmons leaned closer. The caption read, *Bring Hope, Challenge, Reward.* A website below.

Back at his desk, he made a little square out of pens. A prisoner, he thought. I might like that.

The meeting was held in a church basement. Crayon drawings of bulbous heads waving stick hands hung on the wall. Mr. Simmons balanced on a mini-chair and listened to the leader of the reform group tell stories about grateful prisoners getting diplomas, learning Chinese. Mr. Simmons filled out the questionnaire, received his packet, group philosophy, activity suggestions.

And, a week later, number 874569, Sally Baum.

A woman. At a women's prison. How about that?

Mr. Simmons looked in the mirror, wearing a smart dark suit and a yellow tie. He stood at different angles, pointed at himself, rubbed his chin thoughtfully. He stripped down to his boxers, walked back and forth, waved and smiled like a politician. He put on black pants and a tweed jacket. He brought his head up close to the mirror and studied his scalp. He slapped on a cap.

Two guards patted him, swiped at him with a metal detector, made him turn out his pockets. The prisoners were easy to distinguish in their blue uniforms. They bounced kids on their laps, leaned across tables to speak quietly.

A guard touched a woman's arm and pointed at Mr. Simmons. She walked over, thirty, maybe. Thirty-five. Sat down in front of him. She wasn't pretty. An amorphous sexual fantasy about a helpless beauty and himself, hatted, faded.

"I'm Mr. Simmons from the Prisoner Reform Association," he said.

"You got any stamps?" she asked.

"I have some at home," he said. "I could send some."

"That'd be great," she said. "I could use some stamps."

"I'll send some."

She fiddled with her hands in her lap.

"Cigarettes?" she asked.

"I don't smoke," he admitted. He cleared his throat.

She stared at him from under ragged bangs. "I'm in for drug possession. I've got two more years."

He was relieved. He believed vaguely in drug legalization. "I'll send those stamps," he said.

I wonder if she likes to read, he thought as he watched the steel gate clang behind her.

In the week between the first and second visit, Mr. Simmons compiled a list of books. He consulted his library, strained to remember the college classics. I could help her round out her education, he thought.

He called his elder daughter to ask if she had any ideas about books he should add. He read the list to her over the phone.

"A Latin grammar?" she repeated.

"Once she knows the roots, any romance language—"

She interrupted with a sigh.

He crossed out *Latin* and wrote *Spanish*. He called his younger daughter to ask her opinion.

"Why didn't you ever give me a reading list?" she said.

"I'm sure I did," he said. "I suggest books all the time."

"No, Dad," she said. "You always act like I just spit on the floor."

Mr. Simmons was deeply offended.

"See? You're doing it now. I can hear through the phone. I just spit on the floor."

Mr. Simmons brought cigarettes. He wasn't allowed to bring in paper, so he memorized the reading list and recited it.

"Which one do you like best?" she asked.

"I didn't put my favorites on the list," he admitted. "They're a bit difficult. Marcel Proust. Thomas Mann."

"I'll take those," Ms. Baum said. She reached for a cigarette.

He went home and found his wife in the kitchen fixing dinner.

"She wants to read Proust," he said. "I think she's quite bright."

His wife stopped chopping onions and stared at him.

"I wonder if she went to college," he said.

She switched on the food processor.

Mr. Simmons asked Ms. Baum about the book he had sent from the bookstore. "It's all right," she said. A little wheedling and he discovered she had only a high school diploma.

"How would you like to take a college class?" he asked. "Something simple to start, like composition or beginning math." He paused, gathered courage. "I'd be happy to pay for a correspondence course."

She spun the pack of Camels in a circle.

"You can think about it," he said.

"Math."

Mr. Simmons had to admit: something about the prison was satisfying, like crossing items off a list, or winning at backgammon. He learned the visitors' rules, told them to his wife, chuckling. He could have nothing in his pockets, he said. No wallet, no keys, no pens. Only unopened cigarette packs and quarters for the vending machine. And no blue shirt on visiting day. They might confuse him with a prisoner, he supposed. Books could be sent only directly from a bookstore, new. She couldn't receive maps, not even of France. In case she dug a hole to Europe.

Ms. Baum kept careful track, could quote the rules like a sports announcer. "We're allowed three electronic appliances in our rooms. I've got a TV and a heating pad—for my back, you know," she said. "A DVD player would make the third. If I had one."

Mr. Simmons visited Ms. Baum on Sundays. On Tuesdays, he sent her stamps and enclosed notes with them, perfunctory little letters, lists of ideas to consider, practical matters she might attend to. If she was beginning college, she ought to think about a major. If she would be released in two short years, she should think about employment opportunities. Did she have a social security card? Did she remember how to fill out a job application? He had taken the liberty of printing out some sample job applications for her to practice on. *See pages enclosed,* he wrote.

At visits, they talked about the letters.

"Those job applications," she said.

"Yes? Did you have a look at them?"

"What do I say when they ask if I committed a felony?"

"In my opinion," he said, "impolite questions don't deserve a response."

Ms. Baum found her correspondence class difficult. Percents stumped her. Fractions made her panic. Mr. Simmons helped her as much as he could without using pen and paper in the visiting room. Finally he ordered his own copy of the book and wrote some of the exercises for her. Sent them in the mail.

He wrote her about the technical media company he worked for. *I personally invented all their digital filing systems,* he wrote. *Where would they be without my organizational expertise? In a very messy corner, I can assure you.* He wrote about his wife and children, about the time he sent his youngest to France. *Poor little thing was scared, only fourteen. She didn't speak the language. She refused to go, made a big to-do with a social worker at school. But I made her. Who complains about going to France? She had a wonderful time* and *learned French. But ever since,* he wrote wistfully, *she's snubbed me like an ugly suitor. Was I wrong?*

He emailed copies of the letters to his daughters. "Perhaps

you should write to Ms. Baum," he suggested when they called. "She needs contact with the outside."

"When was the last time you wrote me a letter?" the older one said.

"It was Spain, Dad, not France," the younger one said. "I speak Spanish. God."

He was pleased: they had called to talk to *him*.

Ms. Baum told him stories about her ex-husband, who introduced her to drugs, and her baby girl, not a baby anymore, eight years old, in Florida with an ex-boyfriend's mother. Did she have any brothers or sisters? She had a brother. "He shot himself. A few months after I was arrested. I didn't get to go to the funeral."

Mr. Simmons shook his head, patted her hand shyly.

He sent Ms. Baum piles of books, all his favorites. He reread them, jotting notes on a yellow pad, ideas they might discuss. Along with his usual letters and stamps, he sent cartons of cigarettes, tins of fancy crabmeat, boxes of chocolates, and, a few times, cash for her to spend at the canteen. He lay in bed and dreamed. A parade of Ms. Baums marched down the avenue, held aloft diplomas, books and violins, aprons and rakes. Reunited loved ones waved to cheering crowds. At the podium, the original Ms. Baum introduced him. Mr. Simmons spoke, shook hands with the governor. His wife and daughters stood to the side, smiled for the cameras.

Then one Sunday, he arrived at the prison and Sally Baum was gone.

"Released," said the guard at the front desk.

"How can she be?" Mr. Simmons asked. "She had another year and two months . . ."

"Released."

Mr. Simmons turned, gaped-mouthed, and looked behind him at the long line of boyfriends and mothers with more claim to be here than he. He squared shoulders and jaw and marched past them.

At home, his wife was out, hadn't left a note. He called the Reform Association. "My prisoner is gone. Released."

"That's wonderful!" the woman said. "Ready for a new one? We have a long list."

Early release program. What sort of crappy system lets people go without properly paying for their crimes? He took the initiative to write the warden his thoughts. *How do we expect our criminals to learn respect for a government that says one thing and does another? Human law is not God's law. It is not based on grace and forgiveness but on transaction and fulfillment of contract,* he wrote on his new Reform Association letterhead. *I assure you Ms. Baum will want to finish her sentence on principle. She will not walk with dignity given the present circumstances. When you hear from Ms. Baum, tell her I must speak with her.*

There was no trace of her online. If she had stayed in the area, she clearly wasn't taking the bus. She didn't have a job in any of the convenience stores nearby, but Laura Baum and Larry Baum, both unrelated, did, along with several women who looked vaguely like her. In a parking lot, one woman screamed when he grabbed her arm.

She might have returned the books, sold the stamps, made a fortune, and split for New Guinea. He'd be getting a message any day now: *The sailboat is ready. Come . . .* Would he leave his wife and children? Certainly not. She'd have to return before he'd even speak to her. After all I've taught you, he'd say, shaking his head, at least *that* you should know.

Or perhaps she watched him each morning as he left for work, stood with her back against the bricks, peered around the corner as he stepped off the curb. One day she'd step out, appear before him. Why, it's Ms. Baum, he'd say to her shy smile. Each morning he paused on the front step, rocked on his heels, whistled, waited.

He drove to the small town in southern Illinois where Ms. Baum had mentioned her mother lived. He walked from feed store to grocery to bank. Placed his palms on counters and asked, "Do you happen to know Ms. Sally Baum?" He drove home alone in the rain.

"Heard from Houdini?" his wife said over dinner.

"I'll have you know I'm very concerned for her welfare. I only hope she hasn't dropped back into the drug business," he said. "And I will not put up with this scrutinizing my every move."

He didn't think it strange to hire a private investigator. After all, anything might have happened. She might have fallen into a ditch, could be lying there now. She might have hit her head, been kidnapped—Lord knows what lunatic friends of her dead brother might be out prowling the streets. After all, he thought, scanning Ms. Baum's prison Christmas photo into a file, what function does man serve other than to ensure his charges do not topple out of windows or off bridges? After all, he thought when the email came (Logan Diner, four-to-midnight shift, back-door exit), a man must keep track of his charges' coordinates on this wretched lonely tossing sea. After all, he thought, trembling in his light coat, foot planted, near to midnight by the back-door dumpster, it isn't as though he specifically told her to contact him in the event of release. It isn't as though they had a plan.

The door swung open. An irregular rectangle of light, then she stepped out.

"Sally."

She started. "Mr. Simmons!" She wore a beige uniform, tugged a jacket around her. "You gave me a scare. What are you doing here?"

"I've been looking for you."

"You have?" She looked up and down the alley. "You want money."

His mind went blank. "Money?"

"For the books and stamps."

"Sorry?"

"I know I owe you."

"No. No."

"Oh," she said. Her eyes narrowed. "Then what do you want?"

Suddenly he was very small. He was way down there by the dumpsters, barely recognizable—a man in a coat, hands in his pockets, a plain, dull woman before him. The man lifted his hands, stepped forward, said, "No, you don't understand."

The First Full Thought of Her Life

There is a place where a fake river runs along the edges of the parking lots, lots that stretch a mile, asphalt poured out over the earth with the whole resort crunched down on top—planted trees, swimming pools, a store that sells snacks, liquor, and a small selection of wines.

And a family (mother, father, girl, baby) driving away from it toward the dune.

Her dream had been to go there, the whole time she was pregnant, each time, she imagined it, how they'd all climb the sand dune, how they'd stand in the sun at the top, the breeze, the lake in the distance, the photo they'd bring home of their hands raised in triumph.

They'd lost the rental car in the lot and almost didn't make it, found the car, couldn't find the exit, couldn't find the road, found the wrong road, found the right road, arrived finally. The parking lot was half-full. The dune was so white it looked like aluminum. A flawless day.

The shooter was already in position at this point.

The father pulled the visor down and said that a dune is a pile of sand on a parking lot. He said that people wrote books, created myths, invented whole philosophies, about trudging uphill in hot sand, the futility of such an enterprise.

He said that sand works like a microwave, cooks you from the inside through its reflective properties.

He said that a glacier dropped this stuff down here and left ten thousand years ago. Sand is unhygienic, full of prehistoric infection.

He was out of the car now, frowning into the backseat and attempting to dislodge the baby from her car seat. The little girl said that pee is unhygienic and the father agreed.

But the mother had climbed this same dune as a child. And now she'd brought her own family here, on a mission of making memories for her daughter, hopefully ones as good as the best of her own, and this dune had been among them. You couldn't drive right up to it back then. You hiked a path through sandy woods. None of that was here anymore but you could still go up and come down. The same sand carried away on the bottoms of your shoes.

The shooter was in a silver pickup, '13 or '14, green license plates (Colorado?), first letter Y. The mother and girl walked around the shooter's fender and started up the dune.

Three miles away a dozen families were waiting for the boat ride. A tour of tiny islands seen from afar.

Two miles away a dozen families were creating devastation by the pool: pieces of meat and bread, toys that made strange noises, hairpins and spilled drinks, smeared ketchup, tiny stray shoes, wads of napkin, towels tossed onto chairs, strollers overturned, french fries on the ground, and the families—in swimsuits, T-shirts, floaters—parading over the cement toward the water.

The shooter's primary weapon lay across his lap, a Bushmaster AR-15 semiautomatic rifle. He also had a 12-gauge sawed-off shotgun for short range, if necessary.

E had used a 12-gauge sawed-off shotgun.

D had used an Intratec 9mm semiautomatic handgun attached to a strap slung over his shoulder.

N had used such an inferior weapon as to be almost adorable, but that was in 1967.

L had brought 6,300 rounds of ammunition, which seemed either paranoid or optimistic, or like showing off.

W had used an AK-47-style assault weapon with a thirty-round magazine.

Y had had a multitude of weapons: an AR-15, a Glock, a SIG Sauer handgun.

F and C had had sawed-off weapons thirty years old. They'd had bombs and knives, a real showdown.

White sand. The angle was steep. There'd be nowhere to run. And sand is heavy. It would all be in slow motion. Keatonesque.

It was hard to climb in the sand. The mother hadn't counted on that. Halfway up she paused, stopped to catch her breath, and started again. When they were almost to the top, she stopped again, sat down in the sand. (She'd been up half the night [again] with the baby and then couldn't fall back asleep, and she'd sat on the floor in the bathroom like a drunk.) You go, she said to the girl now. I'm right here. It was only a few yards really. Below, the father was walking gingerly toward the dune, arms out as if he were holding a grenade, because the baby was alert but not yet screaming.

Green cargo pants, a black T-shirt that read *Don't Shoot,* a black cap, bill forward, which he'd now taken off and put on the seat beside him. He spotted the girl, a lone child, staggering, her belly protruding, the sand forming a wave to lift her and gently undulate her higher. The girl, and the shooter raising his weapon.

Oh, the layers under the surface (he thought), the air pockets, the parallel worlds, the possible futures that could explode out of this moment, the pasts that didn't come to pass: they continue to spin themselves out until they run into concrete and unspool where they are, spilling into the gaps, gathering around him as he lifted his rifle.

Oh, the inaccessible inner lives all around us (thought some birds going by above), the lives we can't imagine, the water world, the dominion of the insects, the plants, the antediluvian conscious-nesses, made up of light and dark, moist and dry.

There is how time doesn't work the way we think it does (thought the baby), or space either, the scientists have it all wrong and someday we will know this, or someone will, but in the mean-time, the wrong way and the real way run alongside each other, along with all the other rejected theories going back through history, the lives of the baby and the father running along them, strings of frayed yarn.

There is how people think their lives are one thing but they are wrong (thought the father). They think they know the world. What entitled, self-satisfied assholes.

Ahem. The mother would just like to chime in at this juncture, if all parties have quite finished philosophizing? If she wouldn't be interrupting anything urgent? If everyone isn't too *busy?*

(Ummmm, sure.)

Did her husband just propose that she has an illusion of certainty? Did he just suggest she thinks she "knows the world"?

(Ummmm.)

And you, shooter, did you assume you'd be *introducing* something to this family by flattening the girl out dead and bloody right before their eyes?

(Well, surely it'd be a shock.)

In fact there'd already been a "shooter" introduced to this family.

(There had?)

Her husband, shot as a child in the head.

(The father below, the one who's afraid of sand, he'd already been shot?)

Lived anyway.

(In the *head?*)

It had been a break-in. *His* mother had been unable to protect him. Picked off at five years old. World is full of danger.

(And he was fine, the husband?)

Fine enough. No pituitary gland. Those things don't just grow back like a tomato. To this day he had to medicate with hormones every night of his life or he'd die. Try looking that one in the face, Mr. "Shooter."

(Well, the shooter wasn't going to go for the head. Jesus. The middle. He'd get her right in the heart.)

We'll see about that, Mr. Stupid.

At the bottom of the dune another family was arriving, the inside of their car like a circus: ponies and dolls, a tinkling music, glitter sprayed over the seats along with other less-respectable spills.

Half a mile down the road another father had pulled to the side of the road and was saying could they shut up back there, could they just please goddamnit shut up for thirty seconds while he figured out where they were?

Three miles away a dozen families had waited so long for the boat ride that they'd descended through all the rungs of impatience available to them and now were all nearly asleep, a collection of dazed, brightly colored bodies, possessions dropping to their sides, the smallest faces drooling.

Oh, if he had any notion of the clatter of deaths and broken bodies behind this family. He thought they didn't know suffering?

At twelve she'd nursed her mother through an illness that had lasted three hundred days.

She'd had a brother—now in a grave in a desert.

She'd had another baby, before these two, who hadn't made it out alive.

There had been her grandmother, whom she'd never met, locked up at forty and never seen again so that her father had had a hole in him while he raised her.

There'd been plenty of others, dead, or alive but damaged. Earth is full of them, more assembling and disassembling every day. Among them, yes, this perfect little girl, but she'd been pretty unlikely, considering.

(And the baby, don't forget, if the father might put a word in, holding her up at the edge of the lot, one foot in the sand.)

(The baby, who had screamed for eight months when she was born, before settling into an intelligence not yet seen in this family and frankly a bit frightening. Arranging her blocks in precise rows. Sitting alone in a tiny chair with a book, "reading.")

A civilian version of the M16, tremendous instrument, the same kind carried by F at C, now half-hidden behind the sunshade, impossible to see through the tinted glass, only the tip visible as he cracked the window. His body so tense it felt calm.

And don't give her any lip about privilege. This family holds representation of nearly all the seven categories of earthly sufferings. It earned its privilege through immense striving in the face of grief the shooter will never know, and she knew this because she herself was too busy managing this striving and grief to take an afternoon out and wander the area with a weapon. Did he think she never looked around and thought, What a bunch of assholes. I'd like to take them all out? That is a particularly unoriginal thought. She had that thought at the supermarket every week. She saw a whole planeful of people having that thought on the tarmac three days before. She'd think it right now if she took the time to look around, but she wouldn't, because she was *busy,* unlike Stupid over here. She had other things on her mind. The idea of killing everyone around her was just one little pile of thought in her brain, off in a corner, might get stepped on and tracked around by her shoe. Her mind was fertile with thoughts, all of them growing and twisting and filling the space, filling the sky, most of them more honorable than that.

She'd take this guy on. She would.

(Seven categories . . . ?)

Poverty. Her husband grew up in a concrete house by a swamp. Her husband's family picked garbage to eat and her husband grew up among them. His brother spent half his life in prison and came out with so many tattoos he looked like a comic book.

Political strife. On her mother's side she was descended from a race that had been chased over every continent. For thousands of years her people had had to move at a moment's notice, hide their coins in their hair like magicians. In Europe her people had been rounded up, placed in cattle cars, and incinerated without ceremony. Practically every relation she should have had was never born. The world still despised her race today. Don't think she never felt it.

(Political strife, boff! That's a little finger waving itself.)

And what is *his* ethnicity, might she ask?

Hmm. Brown eyes. She'd been hoping for blue.

Well, anyway, tough guy.

He was drawn by her purposeful tread. When she'd clearly cleared the top he'd do it, her full childish figure delineated by the sky. He could hear the cheers of the other shooters of America, he could hear their voices.

The girl kept climbing. She didn't look back over her shoulder to check that her mother was still there. She believed her mother could no longer see her. The sun blinking over the dune, the sand heavy under her feet, her hat blowing (print of whales and waves), the arc of earth in front of her. To her she was going on alone.

In fact, that may have been the first full thought of her life forming on that dune, a strange sand flower, her mind, blooming into existence that very moment: that she was alone.

She didn't mean *alone* alone, of course. Obviously there were people milling around, struggling in the heat, feet slogging, sliding down as they trudged up. At least two kids in the vicinity were throwing tantrums and another was rolling past her, laughing. But no one was *watching* her at that moment, looking at her.

The shooter was watching the girl. Her mother was watching the girl. Did you think she'd let her daughter toddle off unattended? Child was four. She was only twelve feet away, now fourteen.

A young woman, a soldier in Nevada, was watching the girl through a drone-based surveillance camera in the sky. Practicing. She was scooting around overhead, focusing in on objects, in this case, the girl, to see how much detail she could get. Could she see each of the girl's fingers, could she see the shape of her eyes? Could she see the design on her shirt (little fishes, sea-themed head to toe, mermaids on her shoe tips)? Skill-building exercise. Taking a break while the first lieutenant was gone getting a sandwich.

Her father below could make out the girl's tiny figure. He had the baby, weeping miserably into his shirt, in one arm, and he was squinting under the other arm to see his daughter. Look at her go, the little locomotive—but why was his wife sitting in the sand?

The girl's grandmother at home was watching in her mind's eye. The grandmother always had been a little witchy. While pulling on her Salvation Army volunteer smock, she had a flash of the child's shirt in the sun.

In this moment more people were watching this small, un-remarkable human tread through hot sand (her mind blinking on like a night-light, like an alarm) than many humans are contemplated in a week.

No one was watching the shooter. Maybe this had been his problem from the very start. Unseen man. It certainly was a problem today.

Other things were happening. The heat was too strong—the mother had underestimated it—and the girl could get heatstroke and die. The father was right about sand: the girl planted her next step four inches from a tick that carried a new sand-borne disease related to Lyme. The girl was about to spontaneously develop a deadly cancer (it can happen like that). She could in this moment become someone who would grow up to be an alcoholic.

But no kidding there was a shooter on the ground. He'd released the safety now, he was adjusting his scope. The girl, drawing a bead on her.

A thousand miles away a family was at an amusement park and it was awful. The boy was sick. The in-laws were cheap and wouldn't spend any money. It was cold. They were snapping the Mickey Mouse photo. The father was trying to get his money's worth, exhorting them to "draw on a smile" with their invisible pens. They were all grimacing and the boy had torn off his ears.

Dune. Ridge of crushed shells and stones and evaporated water. Built by air and ice. An accumulation of simplest elements.

The mother. She'd told him all she could to save her daughter's life, all she was able to, though there was more that she could not tell him, because she could not speak it, not even in her mind.

At a certain moment six years before, none of this might have happened. No little girl in the sand, no baby screaming at the edge of the parking lot, or at least not this particular one for the shooter to now glance back at irritably to see where the racket was coming from.

There'd been one night in particular at a hotel. They'd been trying to create a rekindling "getaway" (despite all their debt, despite the baby who hadn't made it out alive) but there'd been a scene and he'd gotten away, left, and walked the dark, foreign streets while she sat alone on the bed and wept, "Don't you dare come back, don't you dare," but he'd dared, and at the time it had seemed like a supreme loyalty after all that had been said between them in that room (though where else was he going to go? she thought six years later on a dry hill, fourteen, fifteen, sixteen feet now from her daughter), and they'd made it through.

Now in the sand the sound in her head went, *Six years later she was walking up the dune with her daughter . . .*

These things happen but one goes up the dune anyway, bare-headed, no bulletproof vest, face opened to the sky, and if everyone else has peeled off—father, baby, brother, and so many more—if you yourself won't make it, you sit in the sand and you send the girl on without you, as you must, and if that doesn't work, you hope *something* will and that one day she will know that to see her in front of you was all you ever wanted.

Will he shoot?

I don't have access to his brain, to all of it, only to his intention and then I am swept out (like a fluff blowing off the table). The sun might be too bright, for one thing, too late in the afternoon. They were all looking dead west. He might have waited too long. He might have to come back tomorrow. He had the whole summer, his whole life, really, before him.

But the girl was perfect, the other shooters of America were saying. The most obvious example in the area of what it is to be human: one's continual encounter with inequity. The marking of that encounter. The world would be horrified by the first shot landing on a little blond girl. Then he'd work down, plucking off the others. Or not. One could be enough. This one.

One mile away another mother was buying them nothing from the gift shop.

Four miles away another father was pulling up to a cabin.

The girl reached the dune's top. She stood in the hot sand, the parking lot below on one side, the lake in the distance on the other, her mother twenty feet down. For the first time she knew what it was like to be her. The foreignness of herself to herself, the surprise of her existence.

He released the safety, winked into the scope, finger trembling to pull the trigger, shoot, send the girl rolling, spewing blood, her mouth in the sand.

If she lives, if the shooter doesn't pull the trigger, later the surprise of herself will dull. She'll grow familiar (or frightening) to herself, then bored (or desperate). Then will come that inconvenient teenage self-hatred, like an avalanche, the worst of it hurled at the poor mother, another entry in the ledger of bad luck.

But the girl would soften later, she would unstiffen over the years, over the decades, by degrees, until one day thirty years after this day on the dune, she would achieve the middle-age calm that is happiness. The simplicity of the formula somehow takes that many years to reach. She would take a trip to Hawaii and bring her aging mother, leaving her own children and sister behind, and she and her mother would have the time of their lives (well, not exactly, but it would have its moments).

And the baby, if he doesn't shoot? What will become of her? Same as anyone, though she would never reach the top of this dune, this particular one. She would grow up and climb others— sand dunes, snow dunes, grassy hills, mountains, slopes of all sorts—but her father hadn't carried her up this one and they'd never come back ("Why on earth would we voluntarily go there more than once?" he'd say), so that would be that. But many

other people would climb it, if he doesn't shoot, nothing excep-
tional there. It's a tourist attraction, after all. In summer season
hundreds of people a day would clomp up that dune through the
sand, take photos of themselves, and go back down. Those photos
would wind up in all sorts of spaces and arrangements online,
six races regularly represented (though the average skewed heavily white and Latino). A mound of sand, sky behind, arms open
in conquest. Something about the light made the people look
fit, an optical illusion.

If he shoots, one doesn't want to think what will become of this
family.

The gun will go off. He will shoot. He must. But here, now? He
had casings all over the floor of the car. He could feel every cell
as the air touched it and changed it. He'd never felt younger.

His brothers, the other shooters of America. He saluted them.

But they were impatient. Stop stalling. Get on with it.

Don't, don't do it, the mother screamed over the dune, though
the shooter couldn't hear her. She'd do anything. Not this one.
Please. Not her.

Somebody, help.

Thirty miles away another family was arriving. Tangled up in
three seats, they looked as though they'd been in that row for
days, though the flight was only two hours. They were wearily
watching a movie. The protagonist on the tiny screen was the
hope of civilization. He embodied all the world's longings and
sadnesses. When he flew away, it got dark, and civilization
waited for him to come back, which he did, barely in time. He
was there to save them.

Just then, below, the shooter pulled the trigger. Above, the screen blinked off. The plane was descending. Out the window the glinting waves were like spilled jewels or glowing undersea algae or floating space junk. The earth was made of water and filled with floating islands of light. They were diving right into the thickest part of the biggest, widest island.

Bride

He came back at last to make her his wife.

Or not exactly.

One thing that happened while Davids was away was the woman he loved met an office-supply-store manager, married him, bought a house in the west suburbs, and then had a difficult birth that resulted in a too-small baby who gradually grew to be not quite too small and then about normal-sized. Davids had, from afar, heard rumors of this baby while it was still housed inside the woman he (formerly) loved, and then its existence was confirmed officially by an announcement from the happy family itself—a preprinted card inside an envelope with a bit of tissue, the entire inside an additional envelope.

So as custom commands he sent a gift in the name of friendship because that is what he supposed they were now—friends—and he put his belongings back into boxes and moved back, not to make her his wife.

Who was she now?

She phoned of all things.

"Come see us," she said. "I'm having a party. Bring someone. Meet my husband."

"I think I'd rather not," he said. "I'd rather just see you."

"I'm a two now," she said. "Actually a three. So if you want to see me, you see us all."

Where had he been all this time?

He had left (her) in the first place because she used to say with frequency and urgency that she might chuck everything at any moment, why, she might run away to the city! Except she couldn't, because she lived in a city and you can't run away to someplace if you're there. She said it so convincingly that he himself ran away—to a small town, if you please, took a temporary job transfer, with plans to come back when she asked, which she didn't. A year passed. He heard stories. An office-supply-store manager. A wedding. The water sculptures at the wedding. They had had pouring water and strewn petals and strolling troubadours. And he thought it unfair of her to go off and take care of things so neatly and quickly, in less than two short years, while he'd been waiting around in that small town. He came back to the city, not because his temporary transfer had ended and he was sent back (it hadn't, he quit) but because he'd been away for nearly two long years—in which time marriage, house, child, etc.—and he hadn't found anything he wanted in that town and had found plenty he did not.

"I sent you a gift," he said.

"Oh yes, we got it. We're months behind in our thank-yous. I'm sorry. We're getting to your thank-you."

(We.)

"I don't need a thank-you."

"I always send thank-yous."

"You may toss my thank-you in the trash."

"But I do want to thank you."

"I feel thanked, I'm thanked. Thank you."

"Thank *you*."

"You're welcome."

Why did he have to sound like such a bully? Pushing her around, demanding or not demanding thank-yous?

In the end he agreed to go to the party and meet the office-supply-store manager and the child who now existed but was still small. Agreed to go despite the fact that everything appeared to be wrong where he was living, dark all the time, more so than in other neighborhoods, and his new job was awful, not as bad as all that, but uncomfortable—unfamiliar people younger than he, less educated, watery coffee in the break room, a billboard for ovens outside his window, a slap of tile on the floor, the usual mayhem on the street. While he was still on the phone, linking triangles on his scratch pad, she said something about the curtains, about choosing them, and what she said was "It's loads of fun."

He did not use those words to describe his experience, ever.

Then she said, "Want to hear the baby coo? Listen."

He heard something, it might have been what she wanted.

"Did you hear? Did you hear him coo? Now he's not doing it."

He drove out to the suburbs, followed the directions the woman he formerly loved had given him and he couldn't believe how far it was and how many highways got involved. It was an immense plain out there, everything beige or gray, rectangles and horizontals, flat fallow fields. Gasoline signs jutted into the sky. He kept driving. He drove until he thought perhaps he should stop on these cloned roads, turn back, return without what he'd come for (her) and with what he'd meant to drop off (present: wrapped square in trunk, containing elementary puzzle). He drove until he wondered if someone had tossed her out here and left and she needed to be saved. And then he saw, pulling up (because he'd finally arrived), that this was serious business because how else could she have ended up on this obstacle-course board amid all the empty landscapes of one's dreams?

He sat in his car at the end of the block. He did not want to go through with this.

Then the woman he loved was coming out of the house, a regular-sized baby in her arms, held awkwardly, looking exactly the same as she always had, exactly, coming over the lighted grass to greet the other guests just arriving, hadn't seen him yet at the end of the block, sitting in the growing dark, low behind the wheel. Was it beautiful, that exact way she looked? Was it not beautiful? He couldn't tell, he knew her so well, had such physical pain when he looked at her, he couldn't tell what she looked like at all.

Witnesses: none. No one looked his way. Everyone looked at the bright figures on the lawn.

He drove right by.

Another part of their conversation on the phone went like this:

"I'm sorry about the way things turned out. I meant to tell you."

"You did," he said. "You did tell me. I got the card."

"Card?"

"You sent me a card. An announcement."

He stopped to get a sandwich. Had to. He'd eat and then go back not to claim her. He could not swallow this *and* the chunks of meat the office-supply-store manager would stab off the grill. The place he stopped was a bar near the entrance of the highway, the sort of place he'd avoided all his life, built of chrome or plastic, a glossy orange square they'd molded down so that it stood on its plot without tipping over like a tinker.

He went in.

There was a wedding party in there, in this sports place, and he sat down at the bar, ordered a veggie-snack.

The bride and one of the groomsmen came over and sat on one side of him, the bride beside him in her giant dress, which she moved with her arms like carrying laundry. "Look at those legs," Davids heard her say to the groomsman. "You've been working out." She reached out and touched the groomsman's thigh.

Davids moved his food away from them and shifted on his stool.

"I'd like to feel those wrapped around my waist," the bride said.

Davids waved for the check.

Then a man who had to be the groom came walking over in a slouch. "What the hell is going on here," he said. "One hour into the thing and you're flirting?"

"I'm not flirting," she said. "I'm conversing."

"Looks like you're flirting," he said. "Oh lord, on our wedding night. What have I done."

"We were not flirting," said the groomsman.

"I'd just believe that from you," said the groom.

"Well, now," said the bride. "There's an easy way to resolve this. Let's ask this observer for a factual opinion. I"—she laid her hand across her heart—"swear that I have never witnessed this man until these few minutes." And with her other hand, the ringed one, she gestured to Davids, who had been sitting quietly, who was just getting up, leaving his tomato untouched, leaving a bill on the bar, was going to see the loved woman, husband, child, house, curtains, and so forth.

One time he had written the woman he (no longer) loved a letter. *I feel like I'm investing a lot in this,* he wrote. *I have to get something back from you to keep this going.* She might have been engaged by that time.

"All right," said the groom, straightening. "Let's have it then. Was she flirting with this man?" They looked at Davids.

"I don't know. Yes, I suppose," admitted Davids—because she was! Although later, after some review, he thought perhaps that moment might have been an opportunity to introduce a diversion, ask how the fine couple had met, etc., what they had whipped up for their honeymoon—Amsterdam? Rome?—that perhaps he might have let the poor groom be fooled for the first hours of his catastrophic marriage, let the poor bride enjoy her few days of pre-alimonious existence. This thought came to him because the poor groom at this moment looked as if he'd been struck.

"You cheating whore!" the groom said hoarsely.

The other groomsmen and the bridesmaids came over and joined as one voice, stood as one body, and accused. "You flirt!"

"He's lying!" she said, but they knew better.

"On your wedding day no less," they said.

Then, in a move Davids didn't quite understand, they led the groom out sniffling and then they were gone, all of them. Left the bride frowning beside Davids in her wedding dress, hand clasped around her shell of champagne. Davids couldn't believe it.

"Now look what you've done," she said, turning on him. She was incredibly young and indeed he did feel a little ashamed of himself but she was the one who had flirted, not him, and she should have behaved herself and he would tell her so.

"You should have behaved yourself," he said.

"Don't you start with me," she said. "You of all people. Look, here I am alone on my own wedding night."

"That's not my fault," he said. (He wasn't sure about that.)

"Yes, it is, and you're going to give me a ride home as soon as I finish this drink."

"No, I'm not."

"Yes, you are, unless you want me to go out and look for a rent-a-car and then drive home under the influence of alcohol and get put in prison on my very own wedding night."

"And where are your parents on this evening when they certainly should be here with you?" he said.

"Not here!"

"I suggest that you phone them and tell them what you've done."

"What, that I got married or that my husband left me?"

He considered this. "How far away do you live?" he asked.

"Close," she said. "Two exits up the highway."

Once, by the way, he had saved her. He wondered if she remembered, if she ever threw it in the manager's face when she felt wronged. Said Davids's name and "saved my life." It had happened on top of a mountain in Colorado. She had gotten heatstroke, had nearly died up there. He had gotten her down, not lost his head.

So he let her get into his car—now he had an actual bride with him with all of her petticoats or hoops that she had under there filling up the front seat and he had to physically move her dress out of the way (which is almost like touching her, which he did not want to do) so he could get to the gearshift. The night was beginning to feel eternal and this really was pathetic, this was bad. He drove out of the parking lot, she complaining the whole time, "You just had to have your say-so. Why couldn't you have kept your mouth shut?" This, while he hollered over her, "May I remind you, miss, that you solicited my opinion? Maybe next time you shouldn't ask if you don't want the truth known to the wider public." They went on like that until she shouted, "Exit here, this exit here."

He pulled off the highway. "Turn," she said. "Turn. Here we are. Stop."

They sat stopped and gasping.

"This is no house," he said. It looked like some sort of fallout shelter, nickel-plated and pulsing.

"I can't go home yet," she said. "I have to wait for him to calm down. You saw how upset he was. Let's go to the club and wait it out."

"What? The what?"

"It's a dance club. Let's go in, just for half an hour, then I'll go home. It's right here." She pointed.

"You said we were going to your house."

"A quick stop. One drink, then home."

"This is not the party bus," he said. "I'm already late for my visit."

"Look, this is your responsibility. I might wind up divorced because of you. Divorced after one day of marriage, who could be so unlucky as that? So you better take me wherever I want to go and I want to dance one dance on my wedding night and drink one drink as a happily married woman and then I want to go home to my husband, who could divorce me because of what you did."

Then she said, "You owe me, mister."

Then she said, "You're an evil man."

He was very hurt. "I would like you to think about how unfair that is," he said.

What he could say: Lady, I have another wife to go see.

But he might as well play the whole record to the scratchy end. "Well, I may as well, as long as it doesn't take too long, because I have to be somewhere and I am now running very, very"—he looked at his watch—"*very* late. Honest to God. Jesus." He pulled into the parking lot.

"And you may keep your curses of the Lord's name to yourself because I do not want to hear that just now, thank you," she said.

The club was worse than he could have imagined or just as bad at least. It was late enough now that people had begun dancing. He sat at the bar with a plain orange juice in front of him because he was not going to show up at the home of the woman he formerly loved smelling of liquor. The bride danced alone in her dress. Still, men started to dance with her. One by one they approached.

Everybody looked a little regretful out there, the bride stumbling a bit, one of them taking her elbow so she didn't topple over. Davids put down his orange juice, stood, headed for the outside—because who wouldn't take advantage of these few colored-light-studded moments to make his escape? Was he supposed to remain stuck to this bride for what could turn out to be the rest of his life? He himself felt a little regretful, a little melancholy, and it was a sad solemn moment for them all. He paused at the door, turned back, saw her, white and streaming. He remembered another time he had left her. They were on a subway, coming home from dinner, and he had jumped out at the wrong stop, left her there alone on the train, angry over a slight.

Or there was the time he had stormed out of her apartment. Or the other time he had stormed out of her apartment. Or another time in the car, in the midst of an argument he had gotten out at a light. She didn't go when the light turned green, sat there while people honked.

Who could want a man like that?

"Oh, fine," he said and stomped back. He took her by the wrist and dragged her out the door.

Now she was back in the car with him. "Okay, you had your fun," he said, leaving the lot. "And now you're going home. Where do you live? Hello? Where do you live?"

And she wasn't answering, because she was asleep.

"Terrific, this is just what I need," he said. "Hey, hey. Can you hear me?"

She was completely passed out. "Hey, wake up." He kept driving. "Is this your house?" he said. "Is it this one? Or this one? Just tell me that much. I'll do the rest." He stopped at a stop sign. The street was deserted. He stared out the windshield. The pavement had the gleam of a coin, houses were hung along their plots of lawn. He had no idea where he was. The bride slept. He called to her again but he did not know her name.

He got back on the highway but it was really late now. Her street was dark, the lawn unlit, though the small diamond lamp by the door still burned. Oversight? Expectation? He knocked on the door and waited. The woman he loved, robed and yawning, opened the door. "It's rather late," she said.

"I was engaged," he said.

"Everyone's gone."

"I'm sorry."

(Pause.)

"I'm glad you came by," she said stiffly, although he could see very well she was more glad he had left in the first place, what with this house and now this husband and baby coming up behind her saying, "Who is it?" The thin stick of an office-supply-store manager, who then shifted the lump of baby and sidestepped in front of her. He stuck out his hand. "Any friend of my wife's," he said and stopped.

"I brought a present," said Davids. "It's in the trunk."

"Bring it here, why not?" she said.

He glanced back into the dark. "I better not."

They all stood, saying nothing.

"I need to put the baby down," said the office-supply-store manager after a while.

Suddenly it seemed as though the whole ordeal was over, though it had hardly begun. Nobody was inviting or getting invited in. Everybody was exchanging a second solid hand-shake and getting a single light peck on the cheek and everyone seemed equally choiceless and drab, the destined meeting pass-ing and fading. Then the woman he formerly loved stood alone in the doorway, the store manager gone off to put the baby away, her light-pink robe around her.

"Let me get you out of here," he said.

"Excuse me?"

"Come on, let's run away. We'll leave a note on the table: *Gone dancing*," he said. "I mean, what would you really miss? It looks like some kind of game out here, like some kind of maze—"

He leaned on the door frame. "My own life," he wept, "is an affliction. My own home . . ." he said, taking her hand. "I know I can be a difficult man."

No, he didn't take her hand. No, he didn't say all that or he didn't think he did, not all of it. But he must have because the woman he loved, loves, was saying, "Good Lord!" so he must have said some of it, but then again she wasn't looking at him as she said it, but behind him, over his shoulder. "What is *that?*"

she said, withdrawing her hand (so he must have done that much—taken it). He couldn't bear to look but he did.

It was the bride, coming over the grass toward him, her dress trailing. Her face rubbed and pale. And he saw that she could be the answer. He could devote himself to helping her, to getting her off the drink, back in school. He would change her. He could force her, keep her in a cubby if he had to, just let her try to get away. And after a few years she would fall in love with him—not impossible. They would get married and move out to the suburbs, buy a house right next door to this very house. And they would have their own babies and name them the same names as *their* babies and he would take pictures at Christmas of his lovely wife and tots and put them in the mailbox of the woman he (formerly) loved, who in this dream had shrunk down and was shuffling in the corner of a room.

But even as he stood between them he already knew his wife would disappoint him. She wouldn't go along with it, or wouldn't think the same way, or *be* the same way, or in some other way it would all be imperfect and faulty and defective. He could see it—he'd be in the wrong house, living the wrong life, hefting ludicrous presents across wastelands and deserts, and in his rage at his marred fate, at her unscarred exit, he turned, raised an arm, to do what? To embrace, to strike?

"This," he said, "is my bride."

4

Husband

If you should have an ex-husband, who first writes, then doesn't write, then writes to the point of absurdity, then refuses to write, refuses to receive correspondence from you, refuses to acknowledge you in any way, denies that you exist, then writes again, angrily this time, then less angrily, then angrily again, then leaves off writing altogether, not without a final declaration—he has compromised himself by writing to you, you should not expect to hear from him again—and if each time you are taken in by this, are at the very edge by his either not writing or writing, are poised on the side of a cliff, waiting to see, wanting to know, which is it: will he not write? will he write? until a little time passes without his writing, and you slowly take a step back, and a little more time passes, and you take another step back from the cliff that you thought would surely claim your life, and another step, and a few more, until you find you are on a path walking the other way.

The Mothers

The idea was to bring the two mothers: 1. The two mothers could help care for the baby. 2. The two mothers could help keep the place clean (rentals dirty so easily). 3. The two mothers never get out to the country. 4. The two mothers could pay (mostly) for themselves.

So that was the idea, except, he noticed, they didn't pay for themselves, and they turned out to be of no help. They did clean—too much, under his very feet while he tried to get two minutes' peace to read the paper, in the very bedroom while he and his wife tried to sleep. No, it wasn't that they wouldn't stop cleaning, said his wife. It was that *one* of them wouldn't stop cleaning—his mother. Yes, he said, his mother had to because *her* mother wouldn't clean at all. Her mother did nothing but stand in the way with her arms crossed or eat bread over the sink or say loudly how much *his* mother didn't know.

So there were two mothers, but really, he figured, it was three mothers since technically his wife was a mother. Or four mothers, since one week in, his previous wife showed up to drop off his previous child and then proceeded to stay for days and days, not cleaning, not paying, instead bossing the new wife, the current wife, around. Picking up the baby and saying, "Oh, she's filthy. Don't you ever give her a bath?" So that the new wife, the

young wife, so young she had hardly gotten past being moth-
ered herself and could herself use a bath, turned to him and said,
"You tell that wife of yours to put my baby down."

That, and the two eldest mothers (his and hers) argued in the
kitchen over soap and dishes and drainers and cups, over food
and hair and beds and milk, floors, shoes, sheets, the outdoors,
the indoors, the government, the law, men, bags, dust, and war
(Cold, Iraq, and the others approaching). And there were the
failures of the younger mothers for the elder mothers to point
out: childcare, of course, being the worst and at the top, but also
thrift, health care, and knowledge in several categories, such as
geography and books and fashion. So at moments it seemed like
two mothers might form a team against the others but didn't.

"You tell her," said the new wife about the first wife, "to keep
her hands off my baby. And also off my suitcase, my clothes, my
hair, my man. Hands off."

"You're just jealous," said the first wife. "You got yours used.
He was mine first so anything that comes from him goes through
me first then to you."

"Does not," said the new wife, the younger, so young she looked
like a child, another child and mother he had to take care of.

"She was never good at sharing," said a mother who would
know. "Never could share a toy."

So there were four mothers total, plus his little daughters (po-
tentially two more mothers)—the one from the one wife and the
other from the other.

His own mother had never understood him. Even as a child, he
had played alone with his Lite-Brite on the floor. His mother
had never wanted to be a mother, he believed—but had any of
them? he wondered, surveying the group. A piece of them did, a

piece of each of them wanted to be mothers. But a piece of each of them didn't. Even this new fresh wife, was she, too, showing signs of not wanting to be a mother? Sometimes. And was the elder daughter, at only eight—was she showing signs of it? Maybe. Was the baby? Was even the baby scoffing at him from her little bouncy, not liking, not wanting the role she would one day claim? Perhaps so. Perhaps they all blamed him, which is why they were all standing over there like that.

He had left his first wife for a woman he no longer knew. She had been neither a wife nor a mother. She had flitted off one night, never returned, and was preserved here today only in name, in script, tattooed on his arm.

There were no men other than him. Even the three poodles, shaky and shaken from travel, were female. They did have a bird once, a male, whom he privately named after himself and who died one morning and lay stiff in the straw of the cage.

He went into the kitchen. He'd been ready for a drink for hours by now, and they were ready, it seemed, to find out the things they had always wanted to know:

Did he call that clean?

See how he was?

Was he ready or not?

Final Days

He wrote and said the friend was dying, that these were her final days, and he thought we might want to know. We did want to know. We hadn't seen her in ages, but we'd always liked her and wished her well. We'd heard she was sick (he'd written us updates every few months)—very sick—and we'd had plans, or at least thoughts, of going to visit. A year ago, when we first heard she was sick, we said we'd pack up the car and drive the four hours to see her, camp out in the living room like the old days, but we hadn't. We spent a year saying, "Let's get on the road!" She got sicker. He wrote and said maybe we could phone at least, send some friendly words her way, but we felt uncomfortable, didn't know what we would say. We thought we could "catch up" but our daily affairs seemed so mightily small in the face of her being so sick. We thought we could email at least, attach a photo, but we didn't do that either. Then he wrote and told us how she was flying to Texas, he told us about the experimental treatment, the chemo poured through her body, her weight falling like stones. We listened and felt bereft but still we did nothing.

Then he wrote and said it was happening at last, she was nearly gone. *Is there anything we can do?* we wrote. *Anything at all?* Well, he said, could we call? She might like to hear us. We determined to and sat there afraid by the phone. We discussed it. How could we call after all this shameful time? He wrote again several hours later—so she was already many hours closer to death—and said, *Maybe you could send her a text that I could read to her?*

A text? What could we say in a text? Imagine what she'd been going through, the tremendous rounds of radiation, imagine watching your body come apart, your ambitions shrinking, your ideas about what you want getting simpler, more elemental, your joys smaller, until they are nothing but a few words murmured after another day of not being able to sit up, not being able to eat, not being able to vomit, though you have to. We could say, We'll miss you, but that sounded selfish. We could say, Good luck, but how much sense did that make? Or, We are praying for you, though none of us had ever believed in God. We are thinking of you did not seem strong enough. Besides, how much could we have been thinking of her if we hadn't visited, hadn't called, hadn't sent a photo or an email or a note? What was there to say? What was left? We wrote, *We are with you. We are there by your side.*

Decorate, Decorate

I'm just going to leave it pretty empty in here, she thought. She wasn't going to have any decorations that bring in mud or require too much tending. She knew better than to overdecorate.

But maybe that was wrong? She decorated sparingly, that's for sure. She left a lot out. Now she hurries to look for substitutes to drag in quickly over the grass, tries to throw out the ones that don't take up enough space and instead puts in one that is big and bulky and requires lots and lots of attention. "Now, that's a decoration!" she says, slapping its side. Can you top that? That decoration needs some effort, some hard work. You can't leave that one in the shed. You can't turn the light off on that one. You have to bring that one around with you everywhere you go. It keeps you busy.

Is this all there is? she wonders, looking at her decoration. It was an old question, one she used to ask back when she had hardly any decorations and her rooms were so empty. She considers it now.

What if this decoration stops working or goes away someplace and never comes back? Then where will she be? She needs another backup decoration, perhaps in the basement. She'll need to leave it in the dark, locked away. But what kind of decoration could that be? She walks off through the snow, her decoration whining and crawling behind her, and she contemplates it, tries to see its future.

37 Seconds

1. The time it takes for her to verify the problem.

2. For him to say that it isn't his fault, and for her to cry out, Well, it isn't hers either.

3. (Mango falls in field nearby.)

4. The time it takes for her to dig once more through her bag,

5. to gather the documents, to count them,

6. to attempt to account for the missing one,

7. to arrange them in a pile,

8. to lament their disarray.

9. For a longing look at the other side of the border: scrub trees, cactus bush, the green of a brown mountain, of a white sky.

10. To consider going back, forgetting the whole thing.

11. His next suggestion, not a perfect one, but . . .

12. Her complaint: "You never understand *anything!*"

13. Both of them, brooding.

14. For her to consent to his plan even though it won't work. She knows what will happen. She speaks the language, after all, not he.

15. The slow walk to the kiosk.

16. For her to lean over the counter, speak into the little mouth cup in the glass,

17. to shove the stack of papers into the slot,

18. to retrieve a paper fallen to the ground, to catch the other ones slipping.

19. The length of her explanation, her supplication,

20. meanwhile he in a patch of dry grass, observing.

21. For the lady to reject their application.

22. The slow walk from the kiosk.

23. For a pause to glance back, to see the vendors over the border—she can see them from here—a man selling blankets, copper mirrors, a woman selling rings.

24. Seventy thumps in the chest between them. What are they going to do now?

25. Eighty thumps in the chest between them. Their trip, ruined!

26. The emergence of a cramp behind his left eye.

27. The emergence of a thought in her mind, the suppression of it, its reemergence,

28. the contemplation of it: it's his fault!

29. He was supposed to be in charge of the documents. He had one small job—

30. Not enough time to figure out what he could reasonably say, but less time than it takes to have said it, heard a response, and shouted something else.

31. For her to recite a list, another list, of other things he has forgotten, on other trips, and elsewhere, beginning with aspirin, ending with umbrella, and all the items in between—birthdays, promises, punch lines.

32. Four blinks from him, seven from her (watery eyes).

33. For it to register that he is insulted, for him to comment on the insult, that he is insulted like this often.

34. (A vulture drifts by overhead. Mountains, low red sky.)

35. The time it takes to go from being depossessed to repossessed (as in: car) of the missing document. He suddenly remembers it's in his suitcase.

36. Or decompressed, an exhalation of relief (an in: air mattress),

37. or pressed (olives), two halves of a suitcase back together,

38. or possessed by an urge to forgive,

39. or compressed (as in: compression of the brain [1% compression of a brain]), any lingering resentments, squashed, shoved down in there hard.

40. The apology (forlorn cows standing around, military police a few meters off): she didn't mean it, she loves him, he is wanted.

41. The slow walk back to the kiosk.

42. To place a happy coin in the palm of a nearby boy.

43. The sight of two tourists limping off before the boy looks away.

Interview

I can't promise you that my next book will be published or, if it is, that anyone will read it or like it or like me, or that anyone will review it, or if someone does review it, that they won't hate it and make humiliating insults that will reflect not only on me and my work, but also on you and your institution (should you hire me), and that this won't damage me, possibly permanently, so that instead of the confident woman you see here before you, you have an emotional cripple on your hands who will look sad-faced as she walks down your hallways and will secretly sit in a dim room and watch enormous amounts of TV and lose interest in the work you have assigned her, and be bitter and resentful and increasingly unkind, and then seem to disappear entirely for at least a year—but in fact be taking long walks far from the grounds of your institution, learning about plants, volunteering at the shelter, falling in love with a man whom she meets there, another volunteer, a doctor, and then I will go away with him on a long trip to a foreign land.

Flaws

They went through every family relation they could think of, all that was wrong with each one. They ranked them according to most embarrassing or annoying features—the one who talked too much, the one who reddened when drunk, the one who demanded to be retrieved from the airport. When they ran out of casual insults, they dug deeper—the one who might be on the autism spectrum, the one who was mouthy to her kids—and they spread further—their friends: the bores, the louts, how loud their friends were, how they seemed to be always around. They joked about one of the friends coming to live with them and shrilled with laughter. And when they exhausted that, could think of no one else to criticize and nothing more ill to say, they turned on each other, pointing out their flaws, and they screamed.

The One Fondly Mentioned

Every time we speak, she and I, she talks about her other friends. She repeats conversations, tells me how long she talked to each on the phone. She says cheery things about them. "What I admire about Sue is the way she can take criticism," she says, or "It's so important to have someone to confide in and Mary is that person for me." She talks about them in a certain tone that's warm and nice and that makes one think Sue or Mary must be very agreeable. Sometimes I happen to know the friends she's talking about, because they are friends of mine, too, and I think, What's the fuss? I can listen as well as them, I can take a crack on the head. She's not my favorite person but still I wonder whether or not she talks that way about me. We laugh about something and I think, Will she mention this funny joke I made the next time she talks to Mary? I doubt it and then I feel resentful that I'm not the one fondly mentioned. I think I ought to be, not Sue. Yes, Sue is prettier than me, but I'm more independent, which is a more interesting, or at least a more mentionable, quality. On the other hand, I complain a lot, which is not interesting or mentionable, while Mary is sugar-tongued and therefore more of all of those qualities.

Then I decide it doesn't matter what sort of qualities I have, but what sort of qualities I have to *her*. I court her. I call often, have long conversations with her, and I make intriguing remarks about the intriguing remarks others have made that she mentions. I bring her takeout—her favorite—when she's sick, so she'll call the others and say "that sweet friend" and my name. I wonder later if she told anyone else. There isn't any real way of knowing. I try to think of ways to draw out the truth: did she or did she not talk about me in that nice tone? "I saw Mary on the street," I say. "I didn't know if you had mentioned about when you were sick." "What about it?" she says.

One time, I know she had to mention me. Once, she sank into a deep depression that dragged on for weeks and weeks and finally people stopped calling her because she was so depressed and difficult to talk to, but I was there, on the phone for hours at a time, every day. I neglected my work, skipped lunch to be on the phone with her. I listened and listened and listened, and she told me about her boyfriend and her father and her brother and I thought, Good God, well, now she'll certainly have to talk about me in that nice tone!

Then she brightened up a bit and I never did find out if she mentioned me. I tell myself it doesn't matter if I never know, because at least the possibility is there. Years from now I might be in a shop, having a coffee with a friend, and this woman could be so far from my thoughts that the mention of her name would trigger nothing, and at that same moment, she might be seven time zones away, lying in a bed staring at a water stain on the ceiling, and she might think of me, say my name. Or she might be low, sitting in her car in the parking lot after work, letting the messages, bills, clothes pile up because *who? cares?* and one night in a bar in a chat with a stranger, she might remember me, mention my loyalty when she knew me. It could happen anytime.

Draft

Everywhere she looks she finds pieces of the story she wanted to write. A shred here, a shred there. She even made an audio recording, though she sounds halting and frozen, her voice weak and unnatural, her word choices graceless. Still, all the pieces add up only to scraps—more racket than song, more stones than statue, more rags than rug, more twigs than nest, more brambles, more dust, more flotsam than mermaid, more failing ocean, more drying river, more coming darkness, more clumsy removal of clothing with a stranger, decaying skin, dreams scattering at the alarm, shifting dots of sunshine on the floor, less alphabet, less table of elements, more stuttering excuse, more racing doubts, more hesitation, drifting thoughts, more spreading universe, more space debris, lost star system, more wheelchair-assisted disembarkation than stride, more botched bloody murder where you're chasing a half-dead deer through the woods and aren't you proud that you almost but did not kill an animal cleanly.

Welcome

I finally figured it out and I said it: "You want me to leave?"

I said this because I did have small evidences. The day before out of nowhere they seemed a little mean, one of them especially, the bigger one, the one who had earlier been my champion. But I didn't understand. I had been having such a nice time. I was bewildered. Why did they suddenly not love me?

Then the next morning it happened again. The big one had an angry look on his face. The little one figured she didn't need to have an ugly look on her face, because the big one was taking care of it, so she could just stand to the side and look on, bemused. But I was so foolish, I still didn't understand. I looked at the little one as if to say, Why is he acting this way?

It finally occurred to me: "You want me to leave?"

Of course he wants me to leave!

"You do?" I said.

They'd been wanting me to leave for days already! Didn't I realize? What was I thinking, to be taking over in there like this, hanging around all day? Anyone else would have had the courtesy to clear out days before.

"Oh, I'm very sorry!" I said. "I'll leave right away!"

They were private people, after all, and I should know that. And I'd been in the way continuously, what a headache for them both! Other people came to stay and they were no trouble. Other people were gone before either of them woke, took over the room for only two or three days. And when I was there, I just expected them to be with me *all the time.* They had no idea I'd be such a hassle.

The big one followed me up and down the stairs while I tried to pack up my stuff.

"You don't have to explain," I kept saying. "I assure you I get the point!"

But the big one went on. How could I not see that he was trying to work? Didn't I see that the room I was staying in was the one that the little one worked in? Didn't I see her working in every room in the house, carrying her computer around like a homeless person in her own house? They needed the room I was in. And he was certain I'd heard them talking about how the little one's parents were coming and how they were going to get no break from visitors.

"I'm going, I'm going!" I shouted, throwing my things into my bag. "I understand!" I said, jumping on my suitcase to get it shut.

They just had no idea I'd be staying there for so long, so unbelievably long, they had to put their foot down. How could they have known that I would do that? That that was my plan, to show up there and stay and stay and stay and be so demanding on top of it? What, with my weird eating habits, my slothful oversleeping, my pedestrian reading tastes, my inability to learn a single word of the language of their country. For Christ's sake! There were places I could stay that weren't so expensive!

"I have money!" I cried. "Really, I have plenty!"

Not to mention—did he need to remind me that they *hardly knew me?* How many times had they even met up with me before this interminable preposterous visit? Aside from the few times that we all ran into each other at events or because of people we had in common, how many times, he wondered, had they phoned me up and made a date to see me—*only me* individually?

"I don't know!" I cried.

Twice! said the big one. And the first time didn't really count because it was my husband they wanted to see, not me. And the second time didn't count either because they wanted to see me just to find out why my husband and I had split. So frankly, said the big one, neither time counted, and, even if they both had, it would not have amounted to such a strong friendship that it would mean I could descend on them in this manner. Get out!

"I do understand!" I said. "Of course, of course!" I said, running down the street, him behind me. He was following me now, raising his arms to the hotels, bed-and-breakfasts, and quaint inns that stood all around us. On every corner, sometimes two side by side. COME STAY HERE, WELCOME, WELCOME, signs everywhere read.

"I assure you," I cried over my shoulder, "I do see what you mean! You'll get no argument from this quarter!"

What could possibly be the matter with me? the big one marveled. What kind of person behaved this way? There was a name for women like me, he called as I ran off.

Boulder

The movers came and left boxes all over her house, like gifts or bombs or simply boulders everywhere she turned, so that it felt less like being inside than out on a rocky landscape. Later she sank into a sadness, though she didn't know why, and instead of unpacking sat on the sofa and watched drama after drama, each one corresponding to one of the boulders, each one a boulder in her mind or in front of her face. In the morning she spoke to a friend and what the friend said made her uneasy and it sat like a boulder beside the dramas and boxes. Later she forced herself off the sofa and went out for a long walk with the dog. He kept pulling on the leash, running sideways, each yank like a boulder tripping her on her path, but at last they reached a field and the two set off through the grass into the sunshine.

The Last Composer

I don't think we were expecting quite so many composers to turn up. We made fun of them when they were out of the room.

One composer heard us and protested. "It's not nice to talk about the new guy that way." He turned to a third one. "They say the same thing about us when we're not around."

He was wrong. We didn't say the same thing about the composer he was talking to. We thought that composer was funny and cute. He made us laugh with his cowboy songs and his English accent.

"That guy is a riot." That's what we said about him. "He's okay with us."

We don't talk bad about many people. But there were some awful composers around that season. Every time they got near we hurried away, holding our hair.

"What if we had to sit next to them at dinner!" we said to each other. "Think how bad that would be!"

"Bad," we said. "Awful."

The next day they did sit next to us at dinner, the two worst composers. One on either side of us. Worse had come to worst: here we were, sitting with the composers.

But it turned out not to be so dire, having dinner with the

composers. They were fine. One was a little worse than the other, but not much worse. He left soon after, went home to whomever he had there—fish, dog, bone. I don't believe there was a wife. Then another composer left, a woman, she packed up and took a bus out of town. Another composer went after her and he didn't come back, though he'd said he wouldn't be long.

Now there's only one composer left, one of the ones we thought we didn't like, but he seems to be pretty nice. He played a few tunes for us on the piano. Sad songs, since he was all alone now, without any of the other composers—songs about lost love and death. He told us that usually a woman friend of his sang these songs with him because she is sad since her son grew up and moved away, just like he is sad since all the composers went away, one by one, and now he's just standing here by himself, the last composer. We wish him luck. "Best wishes to you," we say. "Nice tunes you've got on the piano!" We walk out the door, leaving him there, his pencils rolling off the bench, his scores all over the floor. His notes huff out the window.

Yesterday

The dog and I spent the day in our cages, he in his smaller one, I in my bigger one, and we were quite content. At a certain moment he grew impatient and at a different moment I did, but we were each there to comfort the other both times. As night came on we crouched and listened for the man of the house to come home and rattle our bars.

Abandon Normal Instruments*

Abandon the Mind

I already abandoned my normal instruments. One by one all the useful pieces of me have been left behind on a workbench or at a rest stop in Ohio or on a lunch counter. For some reason I just got up and left without them, although the containers for those instruments are still scattered around my brain, the pockets and file folders that once held information: who my friends are, what sort of work I'm supposed to be doing. I keep looking inside but the pockets are all empty. I tossed away what was in them, and now look where I am—nowhere, because I turned out the lights and left.

Abandon the Assistance

First the computer has to go, and the sheet of paper too. Next, your glasses, though you're blind without them. Then the backpacks and the briefcases and bags you carry around and all that's in them, the files and electronic devices and keys and extra

---

* Inspired by a card in Brian Eno and Peter Schmidt's 1975 card deck, *Oblique Strategies: Over One Hundred Worthwhile Dilemmas.*

socks. Then the shoes that bring you here: you have to admit you have a strong relationship to them and they are normal. They must go. The coffee—that's an instrument. Then the rest of the clothing. Then the family, because you use them a bit, and the friends too. The past in general, but most specifically the few years after graduate school when you didn't know what you were doing and were grasping at any straw, hoping someone or something would latch and take hold—those years: you can no longer use them. Abandon them. Then the helpful mate, he has to go, and all the mates who helped in the past—or didn't help, because sometimes their unhelpfulness was helpful too. Desire, that, too, must go (or is that already gone? for how long has it been missing?). Also, all other deep beliefs and dark roads in the mind. And core pieces of me—work ethic and so on.

We are talking about an awful lot of instruments to be shorn off and tossed. And once they're gone, what is left? What can I write with? With no pen, no story, no greed? I might just sit here awhile. Look at the long desk, the wood patterns on it, unless that, too, is gone. I could float in space, a lone meteor. Who knows, maybe I'd meet up with others like me. We could band together. Form a new world. It's possible.

Abandon the Body

Inside the little cottage I was renting, I thought I might be suffocating, that there was a gas leak in the contraption the owner called a stove. Or I imagined the ground was falling away beneath me, that the rock on which the cottage sat was choosing that moment to collapse. Or maybe I had a fever or a stomach virus, or maybe I was having a massive attack. I wondered: Would I die here? Of natural-gas poisoning or of a stomach virus or suicide or rock slide? How long would it take to find me? Would it have been so bad to live?

Normal Airplane

Surely the wicked lady in front of me—who was so rude to me an hour ago when her seat was pressed so far back that I couldn't move my head or arms and was pinned to my seat like a fly, and had to maneuver over the arm of my seat to get out and ask her if she might raise her seat a little and she yelled, "Too bad!" and "There's no problem with my seat!" and when I said I was squashed, she yelled at me to "Live with it!"—surely she has lost control of her instrument, or abandoned it completely.

Abandon Normal Music

It's what musicians do when they don't know what to do anymore. They take out a wineglass or a handkerchief and try to play their cellos with that. Or they rub a balloon and tell people that this is their new instrument. Or they hang on to the bow and toss the cello, and they play their bow on the radiator or piano or a piece of wood. They make a sliding or scratching sound and this is their new music. Or artists, they do it too. They put away their pads and pull stuff out of the garbage. They've been doing that for so long, it's unnerving—this little segment of the population going around, saying that they see art everywhere: trash bin, mountain, sidewalk, plank, person, disease. Some people find it almost annoying. Why can't those artists let a thing be? they say.

Let it be what it is, sitting there, they say. It doesn't need some human to come along and tell it that it's interesting. All objects are interesting—isn't that the point? Why else would we name it? Stick with your own instruments, you artists! And you musicians too. Stay on your side of the line. Don't come sneaking over here and grabbing stuff and running off with it. You want to abandon your normal instruments? Fine. Go ahead. Just sit quietly there with nothing to play with. Close your eyes. Watch the movie inside your eyelids.

Normal Instruments

Whoever said they were normal? Every instrument I know of is either obviously unsound and raving, or at least what people used to call "not right." They are the sort of instruments that quit working halfway through whatever you're doing, or they suddenly turn difficult to work with, or mean, or they take it into their workings to suddenly abandon *you*.

Or they are the type of instruments that stop working slowly, bit by bit, so at first you don't notice, and when you do begin to notice your instrument is "off," you make small adjustments to keep it working, to keep *you* working, because once you start to do this, it is as good as admitting that for you to work, it must work. So you keep up your end, you make all the minor adjustments necessary, a few more all the time, and each adjustment requires a different type of patience from you. It always seems that if you make just this one small additional adjustment, it will keep working. Soon you are attaching antennae to your head, you are chanting, holding things out the window, you are staying up all night, waiting for it to come home. All this is normal (you tell people). But by this time you yourself are no longer a normal instrument and anyone in their right mind would abandon both you and your instrument for good.

Citizens of the World

The citizens of the world are walking along a path. As they go they are abandoning what they don't need, casting aside their normal instruments, because they have too much to carry. The path is cluttered with all the crap they've tossed aside and that pile of crap grows because they're leaving behind a lot, so much that after a while you don't even see the people anymore, just the hills of crap tossed on the road. Mountains of it stand all around and somewhere, deep at the bottom of the canyon, a scrawny line curves through, people heaving their belongings, which piece by piece they abandon. As you move farther up the line, the mountains shrink because they've thrown onto the road everything they owned and have less and less to discard. Finally, hundreds of miles up, there's just a straight path, people walking empty-handed, with hardly any clothes on, a smock or a pair of loose pants, and at the side of the path an object every now and then—a final keepsake, a packet of Kleenex, or a compass tossed aside at last because the owner admitted there was little point in trying to determine one's direction. And farther up the line, another seven hundred miles along it, the people are barely bodies anymore, they've left so much along the way. You see only shifting colors and thin shapes. Who knows where they're headed, whether the line ever ends, whether you ever come to a point where there's nothing left to abandon. Is there always something?

The Magicians

There were two of them, and I hated them with everything in me. When I first sat down across from them, I didn't know who they were, but then they said, "We're the magicians," and I remembered.

"Oh, I saw you last time," I said. "But you're not really magicians."

"Yes, we are," they insisted.

"No, I saw you," I said. "I saw the whole thing. I read it in the program and I was excited. Then I watched. You don't do magic."

"Yes, we do," they said.

"Not real magic."

"It is," they said, nodding solemnly, "real magic."

"My brother was a magician," I said.

Suddenly they looked uncomfortable.

"Yeah," I went on, "he was a magician, so I know what a magician is. That's why I said you aren't magicians."

"Was?" they said. "Is he not anymore?"

I said, "My brother is dead."

"Dead?" They looked more uncomfortable. "What was his name?"

I said his name.

I shouldn't have said his name, because he didn't have a magician's name like they obviously thought he should—I could tell by the looks they gave each other—and I hated them even more.

"Where did he do magic?"

Now *I* looked uncomfortable. The truth was, when he was alive, he didn't perform all that much. "He worked in a magic shop," I said. "He did shows on weekends." Sort of true or not true, or least not that I knew of. He did work in a magic shop.

But anyway I knew what magic was and these guys were not it.

They put their hands on the table and said, "We're meta-magicians, plus we're magicians."

"All magicians are meta," I said. "You're not even meta."

"Magicians are ridiculous," they said.

"You're ridiculous," I said. "You're a couple of bozos, a couple of clowns."

I hoped I had made them uncomfortable when they went up to do their act, which consisted of them dressing up like clowns and calling themselves magicians and running around on the stage and finally doing a single trick, a sloppy, uninteresting, obvious one.

That's pretty much how it went. Until they talked about the elephant room.

This was later, at the party. A crowd was gathered around them, calling out to them and laughing, but they turned serious.

"Once, Houdini made a room," they said, and they raised their hands to show the dimensions. "He called it the elephant room, though no elephant could have fit in it, because it was a very small room. Even a truly tiny elephant, a baby, could not have come in, because it couldn't have fit through the door."

"But why did he call it the elephant room?" said the crowd, but I knew.

Houdini had called it what it couldn't be, but merely by calling it the elephant room he made me imagine the elephant in that room, made me see it standing there, taking up the whole space, its giant feet pressed into the corners, its trunk curled against the door. It became the elephant room by magic. And since the magicians had made me see it, they *were* doing magic, though in that moment there was nothing real about the room, the elephant, or the absence of an elephant.

Dirty Joke (in translation)

This is the one about the salesman and the whorehouse and how he goes in and asks for a girl. He's got the money for it, so the lady of the house brings a woman out and instructs her to sit, legs spread, on the floor. The salesman's job, the job he paid to do, is to climb the scaffold (there's some scaffolding set up) and jump. His dick has got to land inside her hole. If not, he loses, he goes home.

The joke has a pretty flimsy premise. What would a man pay to do that? It might be better if the girl is a princess who's been captured and these are the terms of her release. The princess version could be the younger person's version, the one to tell to tots.

So the salesman climbs the scaffold. The old hag shouts up, "Remember, you only get one chance!" In the princess version the lady of the house is an old hag because in a fairy tale the things the hero doesn't want are all around and the thing he wants is far away, above or below. So the salesman climbs the scaffold. He jumps, he misses. "Oh hell," he says. "Let me try again." The hag says, "Sure, when you've got the money to pay for it" (which he doesn't, because he gave it to the lady in the last joke, the prostitute one).

Or if not that, then the girl is a daughter and this is the family's search for a suitor.

Or he's a war prisoner and this is a prison-and-warden game.

Or she's a bad girl and she's being punished, or rewarded, or he is.

Or it's a sister. It's a test to see, well, who's a brother.

The salesman goes home, heavyhearted, wanting his sister. He practices. He builds his own scaffold at home. He climbs to the top, takes his penis out, points, throws himself off, falls to the floor. He doesn't damage himself this way. He does it for days. He goes back and says, "Pull her out. Set her up. I'm ready."

As a side note, there's also a joke about a penis that pops. The salesman puts a cream on the thing to make it grow. It gets bigger and bigger and then bursts. The joker could say he put on too much cream, that he kept putting it on for some reason, hubris, say (so there would be a lesson involved), or courage (to teach the brave to be meek). That's not this joke but the two are related.

So the salesman doesn't hurt himself and he goes back at last. He pays, climbs to the top of the scaffold, and jumps.

He does it three times altogether, like most jokes: three bald guys, three lost buttons, three long walks to the gallows. The salesman climbs, he jumps, he misses, goes home, has a sad heart, returns, climbs, jumps again. This time it looks like he's headed the right way, flying straight toward that lovely girl. He's going toward her, he's almost there, and suddenly the bride shifts her hips.

"You missed!" says the hag!

"Did I?" says the salesman, because it seems to him like he didn't.

Here's the punch line.

"You got the wrong hole," says the hag.

Mr. Creativity

If, one day, a man should appear on the campus, summoned by the college president, a man in a generous suit, old enough to have had a long career elsewhere but young enough that it was not yet time to retire, and announce that his charge was to increase creativity, and that to this end he would go on a little tour of the departments, have lunch with the department heads, meet in small groups to solicit ideas and in this way determine how creativity might play a bigger role, then how delighted the professors should be and how eager to meet and participate.

Or perhaps they would not be delighted, but would suspect that the man was there to spy and to think of more jobs for them to do, add to their workload with his "creativity" ideas, or, worse, could decide they were inessential, uncreative employees, and the professors might ignore him as best they could, put off meeting with him, laugh at him when he left the room, loud enough that he might hear a trace of it as his steps echoed away down the hallway. Besides, what does that mean, "increase creativity"? They might call him Creativity Man or Mr. Creativity and stubbornly give him no ideas or ideas that were ridiculous, to throw him off, ideas that he'd then chase for weeks, only to present to the president, who would raise one eyebrow, tent his fingers, and frown.

But if, the year before all this, the man himself, Mr. Creativity, had been living far away on the other side of the country, when his wife of twenty years had left him, his employer of twelve had let him go, and his kids had gone away to college, then he might look to places he'd never lived, jobs he'd never held, with trepidation but also hope. He had not wanted to make trouble, but he'd been in such a low state when his old friend from high school, now the president of a college all the way on the other coast, asked him to come, doing Mr. Creativity a turn in honor of their long friendship, showing in him a faith that he, Mr. Creativity, no longer expected from others and didn't have in himself. He had welcomed the chance to go east, restart his life (by God he could do it—hadn't he done it before?), and, who knew, maybe he'd meet someone, a woman he could grow old with. Among so many faculty living in that cold region in that small town, there must be one who is divorced or widowed, though of course one didn't wish such a thing on anyone.

So it was with this determination—not quite enthusiasm but the sheer human stubbornness that causes those worse off than he to grab hold and climb back into the world of the living, "optimism," one might call it—that he snapped the suitcase shut and readied himself for the flight.

Acknowledgments

With grateful thanks to Ethan Nosowsky, Diane Williams, Clancy Martin, Ben Marcus, Terri Kapsalis, Lorin Stein, John Jeremiah Sullivan, David McCormick, Suzanne Buffam, Marco Verdoni (for "Fear of Trees"), the brilliant folks at Graywolf, Bob and Nancy Unferth, Katherine Colcord, Henry, and above all, Matt Evans.

I'm indebted also to the following publications, in which these stories first appeared, sometimes with a different title or in a slightly different form:

Anthem: "An Opera Season"
The Bennington Review: "The Applicant," "A Crossroads"
Bomb: "Abandon Normal Instruments"
The Columbia Journal of the Arts: "37 Seconds"
Esquire (napkin fiction): "Dirty Joke (in translation)"
Gigantic (online): "Final Days"
Granta: "To the Ocean," "Open Water"
The Guardian (online): "Husband"
Harper's Magazine: "Mr. Simmons Takes a Prisoner," "Wait Till You See Me Dance"
McSweeney's: "Stay Where You Are," "Granted," "Bride"
NOON: "Interview," "Flaws," "Pet," "Likable," "The Walk," "Decorate, Decorate," "My Daughter Debbie," "The Mothers"

The Paris Review: "Voltaire Night"

Pear Noir!: "The Last Composer"

PEN America: "How to Dispel Your Illusions"

StoryQuarterly: "The One Fondly Mentioned"

Timber: "Online"

Tin House: "The First Full Thought of Her Life"

Vice: "Mr. Creativity," "The Magicians," "Welcome," "Your Character"

Wigleaf: "Draft"

Zyzzyva: "The Vice President of Pretzels," "Defects," "Fear of Trees," "Boulder"

"Wait Till You See Me Dance" also appeared in *New American Stories* and *Best of the West 2010.*

"Stay Where You Are" also appeared in *The Best of McSweeney's.*

"Husband" also appeared in *Tin House* (online).

"Pet," "Unlikable," and "Voltaire Night" also appeared in the Pushcart Prize anthologies, volumes XXV, XXVIII, and XLI respectively.

Thank you to the Creative Capital foundation and the MacDowell Colony for vital support during the creation of this book.

Deb Olin Unferth is the author of the memoir *Revolution: The Year I Fell in Love and Went to Join the War* (finalist, National Book Critics Circle Award), the novel *Vacation,* and the story collection *Minor Robberies.* Her stories have appeared in *Harper's,* the *Paris Review, Granta, Vice, Tin House,* and *McSweeney's.* She has received four Pushcart Prizes and a literature grant from the Creative Capital foundation. An associate professor at the University of Texas in Austin, she also teaches a workshop at the John B. Connally Unit, a penitentiary in southern Texas.

The text of *Wait Till You See Me Dance* is set in Adobe Caslon Pro. Book design by Rachel Holscher. Composition by Bookmobile Design and Digital Publisher Services, Minneapolis, Minnesota. Manufactured by Versa Press on acid-free, 30 percent postconsumer wastepaper.